A LO
OF STRING

OTHER BOOKS BY RUTH STOTTER

Little Acorns: A Guide to Marin County Plants
Smiles
The Golden Axe
About Story
More About Story
You're On!

A LOOP OF STRING

String Stories and String Stunts

Traditional and

Original String Figures and Stories

Collected and created by
RUTH STOTTER

With Illustrations by Kevin Coffey

REGENT PRESS
Berkeley, California

Copyright © 2009 by Ruth Stotter

ISBN 13: 978-1-58790-170-6
ISBN 10: 1-58790-170-6
Library of Congress Catalog Number: 2009932684

SUBJECT CLASSIFICATIONS
1. Magic
2. Storytelling
3. Folklore
4. String Games
5. How-To Books
6. Children's Activities
7. Crafts

Cover image:
Philip David Noble, co-founder of the International String Figure Association (ISFA)

MANUFACTURED IN THE U.S.A.
Regent Press
2747 Regent Street Berkeley, CA 94705
www.regentpress.net
regentpress@mindspring.com

⌘

Acknowledgements

I am grateful to Anne Pellowski, author, librarian and storyteller, who introduced me to string figures in her 1984 publication *The Story Vine: A Source Book of Unusual and Easy-to-Tell Stories from Around the World*. I have had assistance in acquiring string skill from Girl Scout leader, Tia Smirnoff, librarian-storyteller Jan Seagrave, and colleague stringers Mike Spiller and David Titus. I am fortunate to know professional string artist Anne Glover, who shares my interest in telling stories and stunts.

A very special thank-you to Philip David Noble, co-founder of ISFA (International String Figure Association) who has generously granted me permission to use his original string figures and stories in this publication.

Mark Sherman, ISFA Editor has helped me to locate string figure directions and his ISFA publications which include Bulletins, newsletters and online string figure directions have been and will continue to be, inspiring.

I also want to express my appreciation to Jan Seagrave for assistance in preparing this publication and to Mark Weiman of Regent Press for his many kindnesses which include publishing *A Loop of String*.

Table of Contents

INTRODUCTION 13

ABOUT STRING FIGURES 15

1. WINKING EYE 17
    String Figure: **Winking Eye**

2. FREDDIE THE FLEA 21
    String Figures:
        Sand Flea
        Moth
        Japanese Butterfly

3. THE CLEVER JESTER 27
    String Figures:
        Neck release 1
        Neck release 2
        Neck release 3
        Neck release 4

4. IF I GIVE YOU DIAMONDS 37
    String Figures:
        Jacob's Ladder
        Two Diamonds

5. STAR CATCHER 41
    String Figures:
        Spear
        Throwing the Spear
        Tree
        Ladder
        Moon
        Star

6. CHOPPING WOOD 47
    Stories:
        Sharing the Log
        African traditional myth
    String Figure: **Chopping Wood**

7. FIREMAN TO THE RESCUE 51
 String Figure: **Ladder**

8. CUTTING THE FINGERS STORIES 53
 Train Story
 Farmer and his Potatoes
 Yam Thief
 Cat and Mouse
 Holiday Story Adaptations
 Uprooting Alou

9. SPIDER'S LUNCH 59
 String Figure: **Mosquito**

10. HOUSE ON FIRE 61
 String Figure: **Siberian House**

11. A KNOTTY STORY 65
 String Figure: **A stunt with string knots**

12. SNAKE'S LUNCH 67
 String Figure: **Lizard Escapes**

13. THE CONTEST 69
 String Figure: **Apache Door**

14. ARBOR DAY TALE 73
 String Figure: **Tree**

15. FROG 75
 Stories:
  The Prodigal Frog
  The Frog Olympics
 String Figure: **Frog**

16. A ZEN STORY 81
 String Figure: **Pouring Tea**

17. BUTTON HOLE STUNT 1 & 2 83

18. RING STUNT 85

19. STRING STUNT FOR TWO PEOPLE 87

20. STRING JOKE 89

21. STRING GAME 91

ADDENDA

TERMINOLOGY AND BASIC MOVES 93
    Opening A
    Your Fingers
    Navajo
    Sharing A Loop
    Palmar String
    Dorsal String
    Near String
    Far String

ADDITIONAL STRING STORIES 95

STRING FIGURES ON DVD AND VHS 96

WHERE TO FIND STRINGS 97

WHERE TO PURCHASE STRINGS 98

CHILDREN'S BOOKS THAT FEATURE STRING FIGURE ART 99

RECOMMENDED STRING FIGURE BOOKS 100

ON THE WEB 102

INDEX 103

ISFS (INTERNATIONAL STRING FIGURE ASSOCIATION) 104

Introduction

Most people are familiar with the non-verbal string game, Cat's Cradle, which is played by two people cooperatively working the loop of string. In other parts of the world, however, making string figures is accompanied by stories, often associated with mythology and religious beliefs. Stories may accompany the making of the string designs, the story, part of the story or may be told after the design is completed.

It is amazing that something as simple as a loop of string can take so many shapes and perform so many stunts. I have found that telling stories and creating designs with a loop of string develops memory, imagination, eye-hand coordination, flexible fingers, and may even reduce stress and bring harmony into your life. Best of all, this is great fun!

> Anthropologist professor A.C. Haddon (1855-1940) had as his motto, "You can travel anywhere with a smile and a piece of string." I have found this to be absolutely true!

About String Figures

It is believed that string figures originated in the early Stone and Bronze ages among Inuit Eskimo cultures. Anthropologist Franz Boas, studying Eskimo cultures, was the first scholar to write about string figures (1888), as well as about the Yupik art of telling stories while drawing pictures in the mud or snow with a storyknife. String figures, the first "picture books", accompanied by chants, songs and stories are frequently associated with traditional rituals and religions — the designs depicting objects, people and events.

Navajo American Indians in the southwestern United States, the Maori in New Zealand, the Aboriginals in Australia, the Rapa Nui on Easter Island are a few of the cultures that still include string figures in their traditional life. On Easter Island there is an annual folk festival that includes a string figure "kai kai" competition. Two families are selected for the final competition and the judging includes finger dexterity, creativity and accompanying story or chant.

The Navajo say that making string figures was a gift from Grandmother Spider, an important figure in their mythology. On the Polynesian islands traditional belief is that Maui, the demigod and trickster, introduced string figures.

If you are traveling, learn the word for this art form to learn more about these figures. For example, in Hawaii, creating string figures is known as "Hei" (net), "Koko" and "Makali." In Japan string figures are called "Itotori," "Itodori," and "Aya ito tori."

To find out more about string figures and storytelling see Stotter's article "String Figures" in *Storytelling: An Encyclopedia of Mythology and Folklore, Volume Two*, edited by Josepha Sherman, Sharpe Reference, Armonk, New York. 2008.

#1 WINKING EYE

STORY

A man loved to tease people. He would say things like, "I think water attracts electricity. Every time I am in the bath the phone rings." But they knew he was teasing, because he always winked after he said something funny. Like this! (Make the string eye wink as described below)

One day the man told a little girl about paint that was sold when he was a little boy. "Why, " he told her, "you could buy striped paint. Any colors you wanted. Around the 4th of July the striped red, white and blue was very popular. You dipped your brush in the paint, and on your wall, or bird house, you instantly got beautiful red, white and blue stripes. Then a little later they came out with poke-a-dot paint. Oh, that was pretty! Bright red with yellow dots was my favorite." Then he would wink. Like this. (Make the string eye wink as described below.)

STORY BY RUTH STOTTER

Have fun adding your own tall tales and exaggerations.

DIRECTIONS

(1) Put the loop over your four fingers on your left hand with your thumb on top.

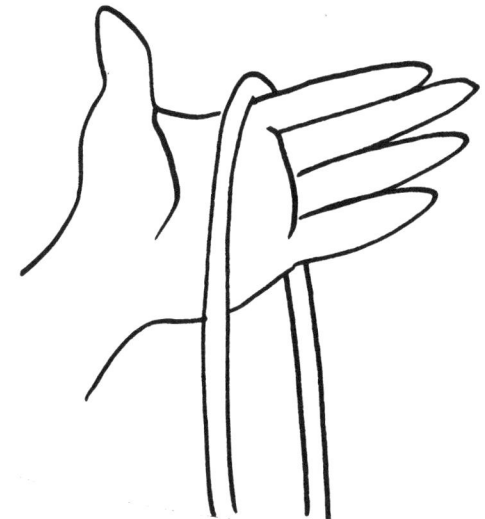

(2) Hold the string down with your little, ring and middle fingers.

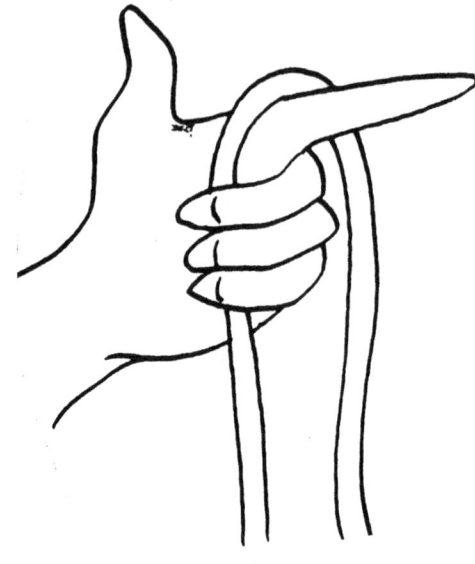

(3) With your right hand, take the string that is falling behind your pointer finger and put it on top of your pointer finger, wrap it completely around your pointer finger.

(4) Bring this string in-between your pointer finger and thumb. It is now hanging behind your thumb.

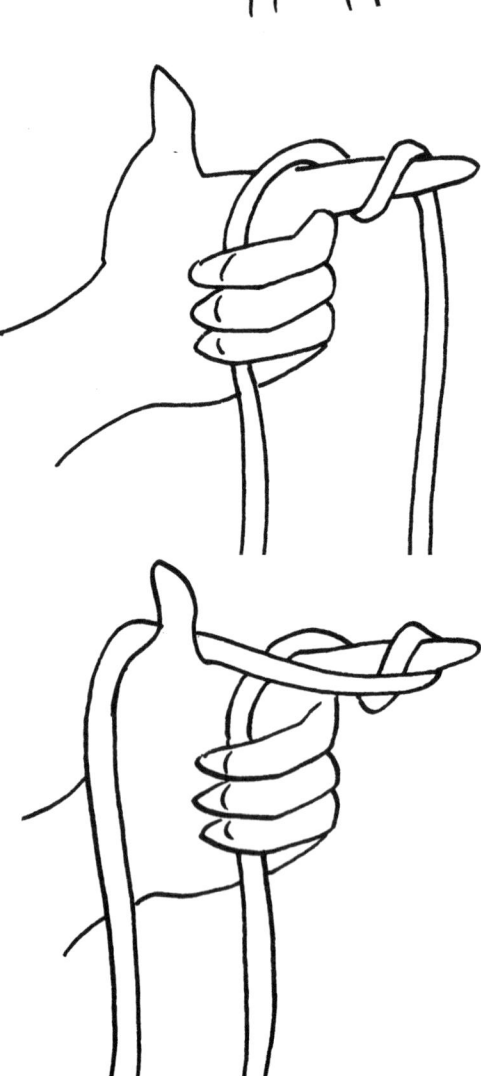

(5) Take the loop that is on top encircling your pointer finger, lift it over to go around your thumb. This is called sharing the loop.

(6) Take the string of the loop that is closest to you, the one around your thumb closest to your wrist, and move it so it now rests between your pointer finger and thumb.

(7) Take the other string, the one your three fingers had been holding, lift it up and bring it over behind your thumb so that it is now lying closest to you (where the other string was in step 6.)

(8) See the triangle eye!

(9) To make the eye wink slightly relax your fingers as you pull sideways on the hanging loop. To open the eye again, extend your fingers and loosen your hold on the loop.

This string figure, "The Wink," was originally collected in Kauai, Hawaii.

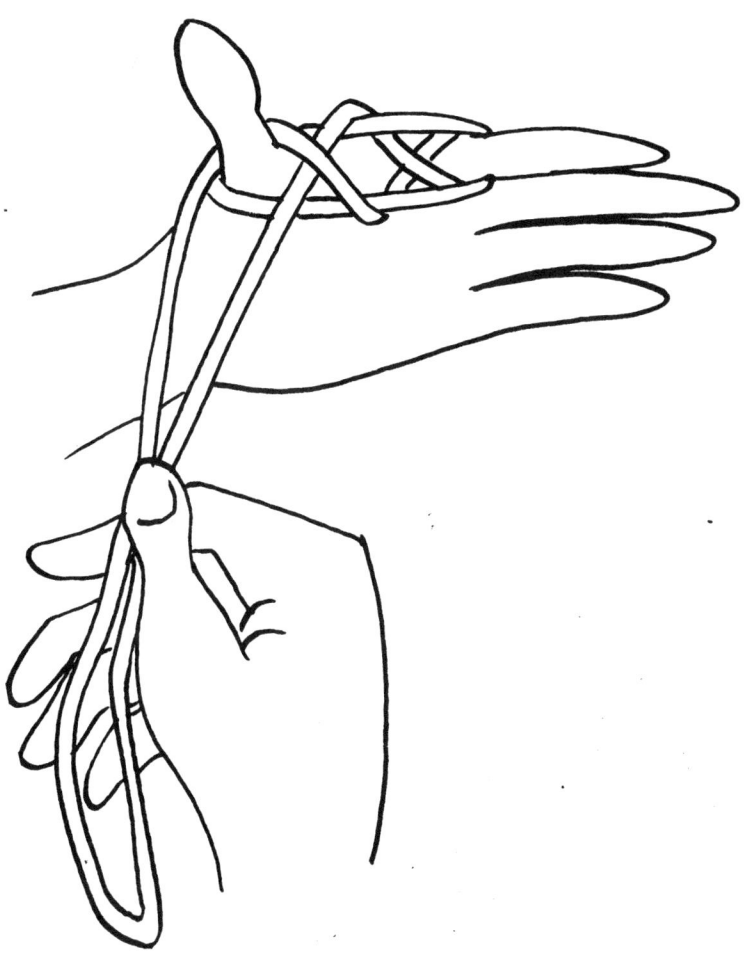

#2
FREDDIE THE FLEA

This figure has a dramatic presentation when created with a multicolored rainbow string.

STORY

Katy Caterpillar and Freddy Flea were best friends. Everyday they would meet to talk and laugh and do all the things best friends like to do together. One day Freddie went out to play. "Katie. Katie. Where are you?" He could not find her. Then he heard a voice. "Here I am Freddie. I changed. I know that I look different, but I am still Katie, and I am still your friend."

Freddie the flea was so happy he jumped for joy. Freddie the flea jumped for joy!

STORY BY RUTH STOTTER

DIRECTIONS

(1) Begin with a figure eight loop lying side-wise on a table, the floor or your lap.

(2) Identify the string that is on the bottom. This bottom string has one end at the top of the figure and one end at the bottom. Pick up this string. As you hold it up, it becomes a butterfly.

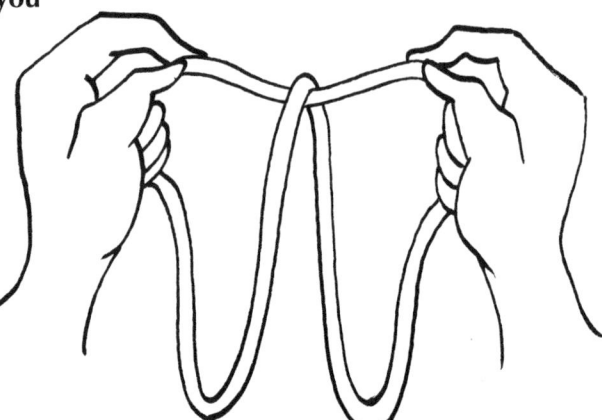

(3) When you give a tug on the two strings you are holding, the center, where the strings cross pops up! The "U" at the top of the butterfly, pulled into a straight string, creates this effect.

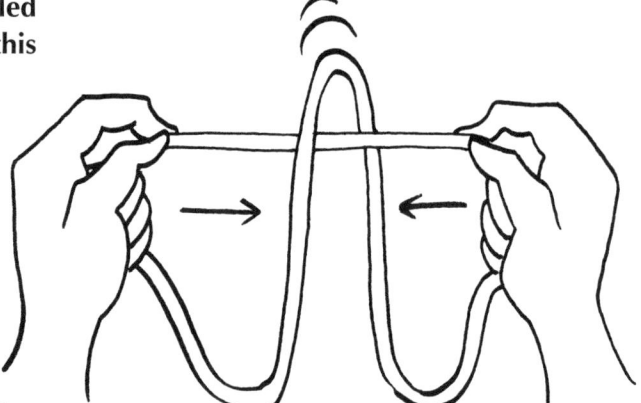

(4) Tug the strings to make the flea jump again! And again!

This string figure was found in *Kwakiutl String Figures* by Julia Averkieva and Mark A. Sherman (University of Washington Press, 1992, page 104). It is called "a Sand Flea" and "Qat!" This snapping string action was also collected in New Guinea where it is called "Fish Jumping from Stone to Stone." In Fiji it is called "A Fish Out of Water." In *Now You See It*, Michael Taylor calls this "A Puddle and a Jumping Fish."

THE MOTH

Here's another string figure to use with this story.

DIRECTIONS

(1) Opening A.

(2) Drop the strings from both thumbs.

(3) Pass your thumbs over closest two strings and pick up the string on your little finger closest to you. (The near little finger string.)

(4) Drop the strings from your little fingers.

(5) Put your thumbs under the near pointer finger strings and bring them back.

(6) You now have two strings on your thumb. Navajo. (Lift the lower string over the upper string.)

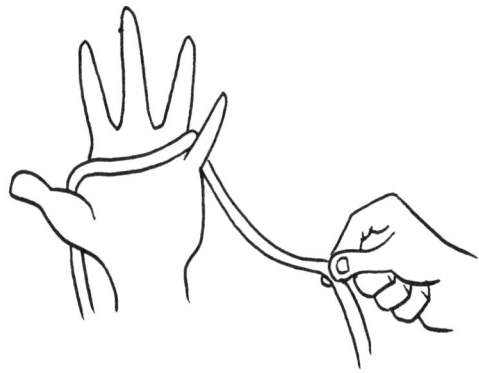

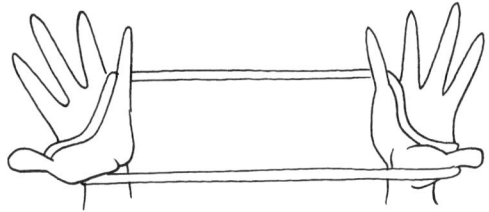

(7) Drop your pointer fingers into the loop that goes around the string lying between your thumb and pointer finger.

(8) Extend your fingers to see the moth.

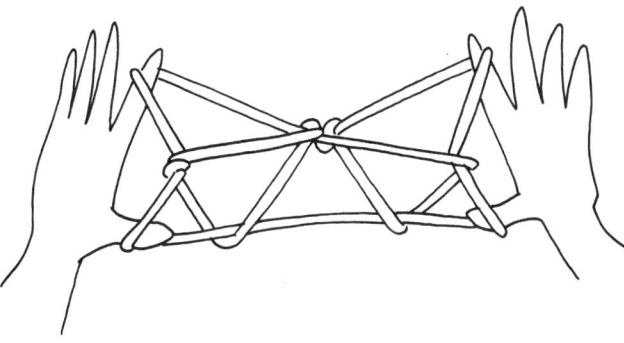

This Zulu string figure from South Africa is also called "Spectacles." You can hold this figure in front of your eyes and mime that you are wearing glasses. You could even pretend that they are magic glasses.

JAPANESE BUTTERFLY

This beautiful butterfly makes an impressive follow-up to this story.

DIRECTIONS

(1) Put the strings around your thumbs.

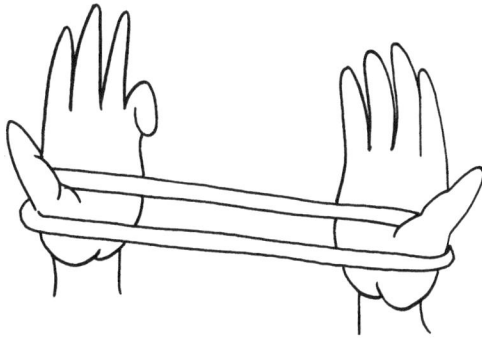

(2) With your left little finger, go under the far thumb string on your left hand and bring it back. You now have a palmer string on your left hand.

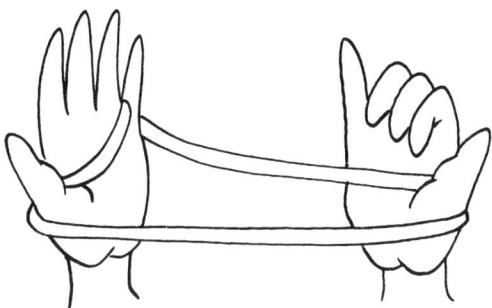

(3) Insert your right little finger into this string that is across your left hand, from behind (diving down in back of the string). As you bring it back, it will have a slight clockwise twist.

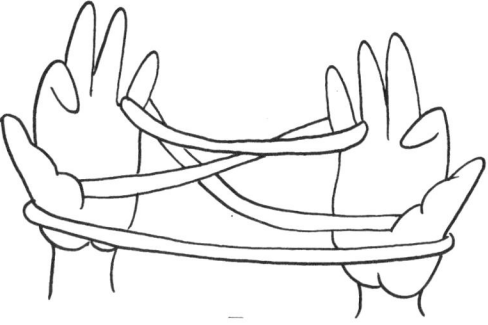

If you turn opening A sidewise, from an up and down perspective, it becomes a butterfly. Emma Coleman, a San Rafael grade school student, showed this to me.

(4) Both pointer fingers go under the near little finger strings and bring them back.

(5) Do opening A, using your middle finger to go under the short palmar strings (it is in front of two fingers) on each hand.

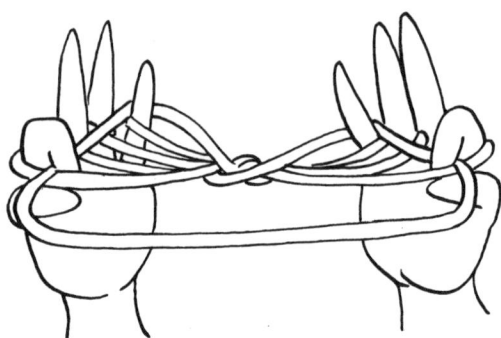

(6) Both little fingers hook the far thumb strings and bring them back.

(7) Bend each pointer finger down to hook the little string that is in front of them and hold these fingers in this position.

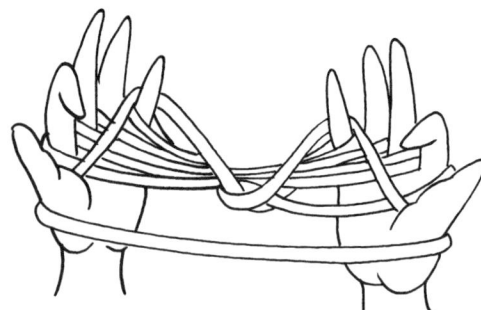

(8) Drop the thumb loops on both hands.

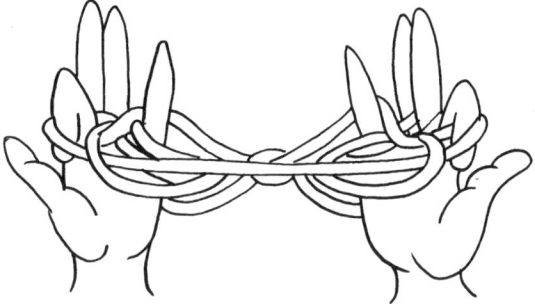

(9) Turn your palms so that they are facing you. Do you see the butterfly?

#3
THE CLEVER JESTER STORY

STORY

The Caliph of Bagdad, angry with his court jester, sentenced him to death by hanging. But when the executioner put the rope around his neck, the jester freed himself! (Do first neck release.) So, the executioner put another noose around the jester's head. But, once again, in a different manner, he freed himself! (Do second neck release.) The third time the rope was put around his neck he astonished everyone by again freeing himself. (Do third neck release.) A fourth time the hangman put the noose around his neck. (Do fourth neck release.)

When once again the jester escaped, the Caliph said, "Since it appears that we cannot hang you, I will allow you to choose the method for your death. How do you want to die?" The jester bowed. "Thank-you. Since you allow me to choose by what means I die, then I ask that I die of old age." The Caliph laughed, "Of old age!" and when he laughed, he forgot why he had been angry with his jester. And they both lived ... happily ever after.

ANONYMOUS FOLKTALE ADAPTED BY RUTH STOTTER

This story, without the hanging interludes, is a traditional Jewish folktale. In the published texts there is no reference to hanging; the King allows the jester to select his method of death. This story can be found in *A Treasury of Jewish Folklore* by Nathan Ausubel, New York: Crown Publishers, 1948, 1975, as well as in *While Standing on One Foot: Puzzle Stories and Wisdom tales from the Jewish Tradition* by Nina Jaffe and Steve Zeitlin, New York: Henry Holt and Company, 1993.

Neck Release 1

DIRECTIONS:

Bring the loop together as a double string and put it around your neck (like a scarf) so that you have a loop hanging down on each side of your neck. Into the loop on the left side insert your left little finger from below. Into the loop on the right side, insert your right thumb, also from below. With your right hand little finger pick up from underneath the left string that is closest to you and pull it in front of your neck while you make a grimacing face and say "aargh" as the string passes close to the front of your throat, creating the effect that the string is cutting into your neck. Now release all your fingers except your right thumb and at the same time quickly pull the string held by your thumb. The strings appear to have passed right through your neck and you have defeated the hangman!

Neck Release 2
And That's the End of That!

Practice this in front of a mirror.

> You can also use this to end a story or performance with a dramatic trick:
> Say, "And that's" as you you put the string over your head and cross it.
> Say, "The end" as you pull it over your head.
> Say "Of that!" as you pull on the string and clap — creating the effect that the string is passing through your neck.
>
> I sometimes ask, "Would you like to see the hole in my neck?" when doing this as a solo stunt. Or you might use this as a magic trick, saying, "I can pass this string through my neck."

DIRECTIONS:

1) Put the string over your head, like a necklace.

(2) Take the two ends and cross them in front of your face, biting the X where the strings cross.

(3) Uncross your hands but do not let go of the strings and do not change hands.

(4) Do not let go of the strings and do not change hands as you lift the string up over your head.

(5) Clap your hands, bringing together in front of you the two ends of the loops you are holding. As you pull your hands apart, the string will have appeared to have magically passed through your neck.

IMPORTANT
- ⌘ Be sure to clap — this enhances the magical effect.
- ⌘ Be sure to quickly pull back the two sides of the string behind your neck as you clap. If you do this slowly, or if they remain in front of your neck, the effect is diminished.

This has been collected in the Philippines and Caroline Furness was shown this figure in the Caroline Islands. It was also collected by Dr. W. A. Cunningham in Central Africa.

Neck Release 3
Cheating the Hangman

Use an extra long string for this stunt. A 70" string made into a loop whould work. Effect: You have a double string securely around your neck. When you pull on the string in front of you, the strings around your neck magically fall away.

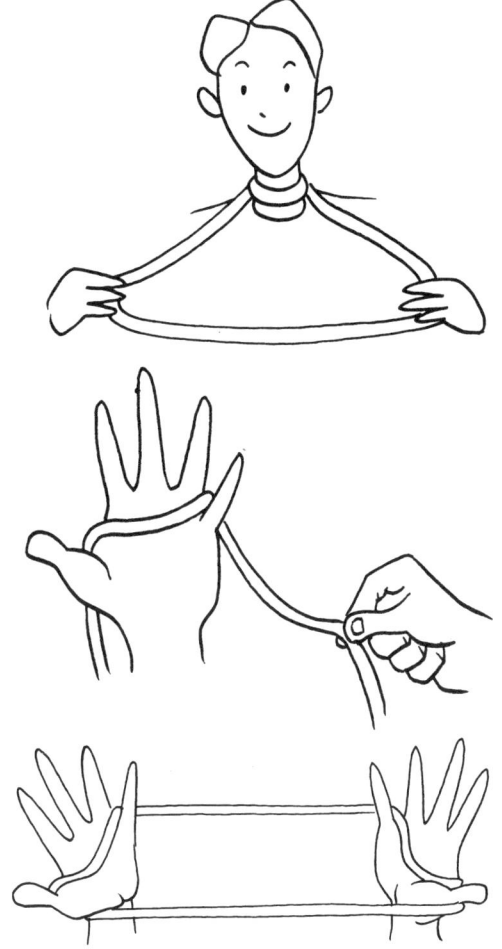

DIRECTIONS:

(1) Put the string over your head like a necklace.

(2) Take the right hand string with your right hand and put it around your neck. Now you have two loops around your neck. Draw one loop tight around your neck and let the other loop hang down in front of you.

(3) Do Opening A. (Be sure to begin with the right pointer finger taking the left palmar string.)

(4) Release the loops from your little fingers. You are now facing two strings that cross in front of you. Behind these strings there is a single string.

(5) This single string must come *under* the crossed strings. Use your little fingers to pull this single string forward under the other strings. Tuck it under your chin.

(6) Insert your head into the loop. (The double strings are at the top of this loop.) Pull the loop over your head.

(7) Release the loops from your thumbs.

(8) Quickly pull the ends of the string with your pointer fingers and the string will magically pull free!

Neck Release 4

This is impressive as there are several strings around your neck. Use a longer string and practice this until you can do the moves quickly and gracefully.

DIRECTIONS:

(1) Put the loop over your head like a necklace.

(2) Put the loop around your neck a second time — one loop is up closer to your neck and the other is hanging down in front of you.

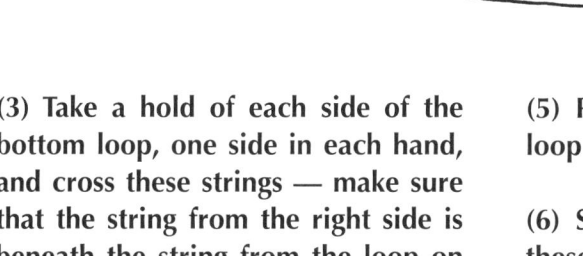

(3) Take a hold of each side of the bottom loop, one side in each hand, and cross these strings — make sure that the string from the right side is beneath the string from the loop on the left side and hold this cross with your left hand.

(4) Now each hand also takes the string directly below it from the hanging loop and gently pull these, almost sliding them, out until there is a loop large enough that you can insert your head.

(5) Put your head directly into this loop and pull it over your head.

(6) Stop so that people can see all these strings going around your neck; you appear to be trapped.

(7) When you pull forward on the string that is up high closest to your neck (from step 2) all the strings come forward. You have again magically escaped.

I was taught this neck escape from Elaine Stanley, a California storyteller, who learned it from Philip David Noble when he visited California.

#4
IF I GIVE YOU DIAMONDS

Here are two string figure designs to create diamonds.

STORY

A prisoner of war offered to give the prison guard diamonds if he would let him go.

The soldier said, "If I give you diamonds will you let me go?"

The guard was excited. "You will give me diamonds if I let you go?"

When the guard agreed, the soldier pulled out a piece of string and — voila! — diamonds.

The guard, an honorable man, kept his word and the prisoner was released.

STORY BY RUTH STOTTER

JACOB'S LADDER

You will make four diamonds

DIRECTIONS

(1) Opening A.

(2) Drop the loops off both thumbs.

(3) Take your thumbs under all the strings and hook the string on the far side of your little finger. Bring this string back, underneath all the other strings, to the front.

(4) Now, use your thumbs to go over the string closest to you and under the next string. Bring this back. You now have two loops on your thumb.

(5) Drop the strings from your little fingers.

(6) Take both little fingers across the string closest to it and hook from underneath the string on your thumb that is closest to you it, the far thumb string. Bring this back.

(7) Drop all the loops from your thumbs. You have cats whiskers.

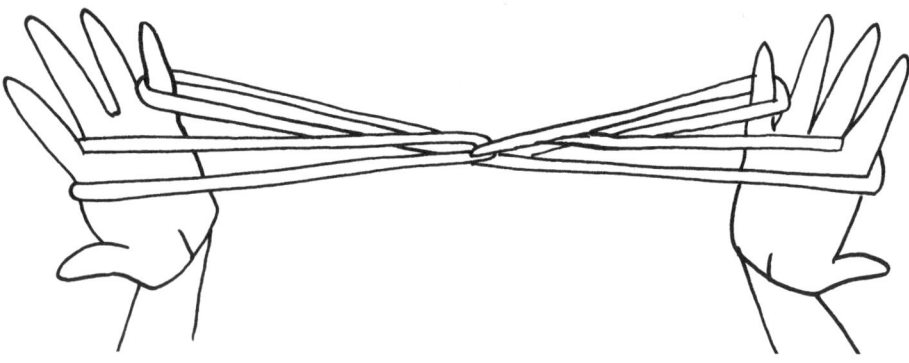

(8) Now, use your thumbs to go over the two strings closest to you and under the next string. Bring this back.

(9) Now you will share-the-loop. Take the loop from your pointer finger and bring it over to make a second loop on your thumb. Do this with both hands.

(10) Navajo is the term for the next step. See page 94. Take the lower loop and lift it up over the top loop. Do this with both thumb loops.

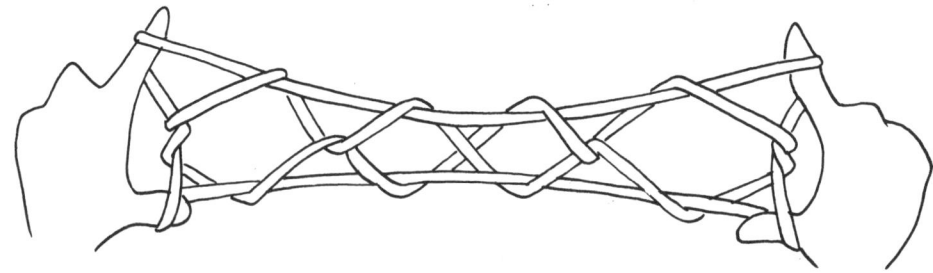

(11) Pull your hands apart, spread your fingers and rotate your palms so they face you. Look for the little triangle between your thumb and pointer finger. Drop your pointer fingers down into these triangles, and hold them firmly there. Drop the loops from your little fingers as you spread your fingers apart. Voila! Four Diamonds!

> "Jacob's Ladder," is called "Calabash Net" in Yoruba, West Africa. In other countries it has been called "London Bridge," "A Hammock" and "Sydney Harbor Bridge." "Two Diamonds" was collected from the Maori's in New Zealand.

TWO DIAMONDS

This is a little easier, and the prisoner can offer two diamonds.

DIRECTIONS

(1) Do Opening A.

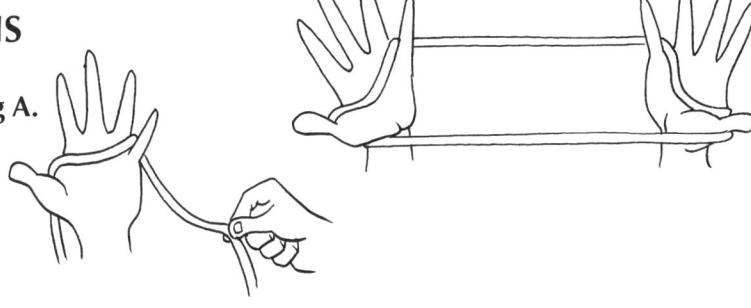

(2) Drop the strings from both thumbs.

3) Take your thumbs across all the strings and bring back the string farthest from you, the far little finger string — on the back of your thumbs.

4) Share the loop. Take the loop from each pointer finger and put it on your thumb.

5) Navajo. Lift the string that is below on your thumb so it becomes the top thumb string.

6) Pull your hands loosely apart and insert your pointer fingers into the little triangles by your thumbs, made by the two strings closest to you.

7) Drop the strings from your little fingers.

8) Pull your hands apart, spread them open with you palms facing away from you to see ..... two diamonds!

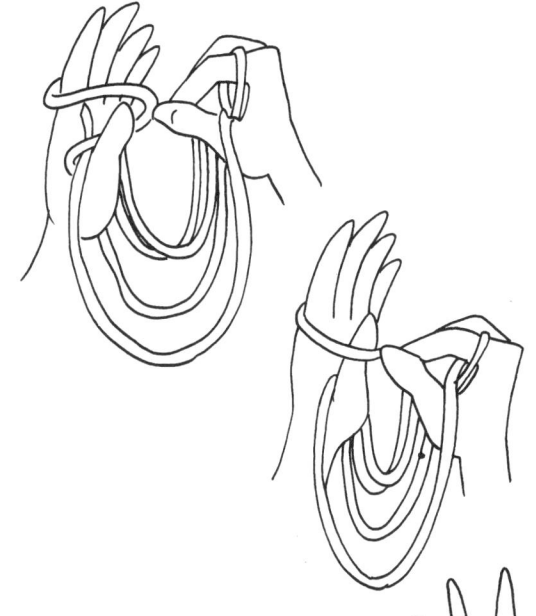

#5
THE STAR CATCHER

This story uses five string figure designs. If you are performing with a group you can have two people make the spears, facing toward each other and mime throwing the spear. Another person can make the moon, another, the ladder, and another the star. End with having just one person make the spear and demonstrate throwing it from one hand to the other. After seeing this done by two people at the beginning, this makes an impressive finale.

STORY

A boy was practicing throwing spears. He threw his spear. He threw it again. But this time the wind carried his spear up, up, up — all the way up to the moon. It was a full moon and he could see his spear. The boy climbed a tree to try to reach his spear. But when he reached up, he caught, not the moon, but ... a falling star! If you want to know if this is a true story, look at the full moon. If you look carefully, you might see the man on the moon throwing that spear back and forth, back and forth.

STORY BY RUTH STOTTER

TO MAKE THE SPEAR

(1) Do opening A (starting with the right finger.) See page 93.

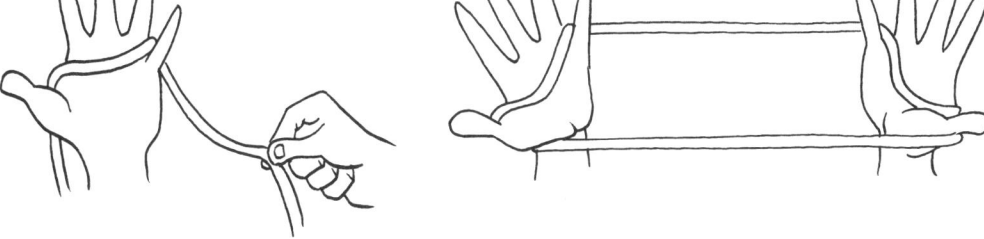

(2) Next, put your left pointer finger loop on the right pointer finger and take the loop from the right pointer finger on to your left pointer finger. Separate your hands.

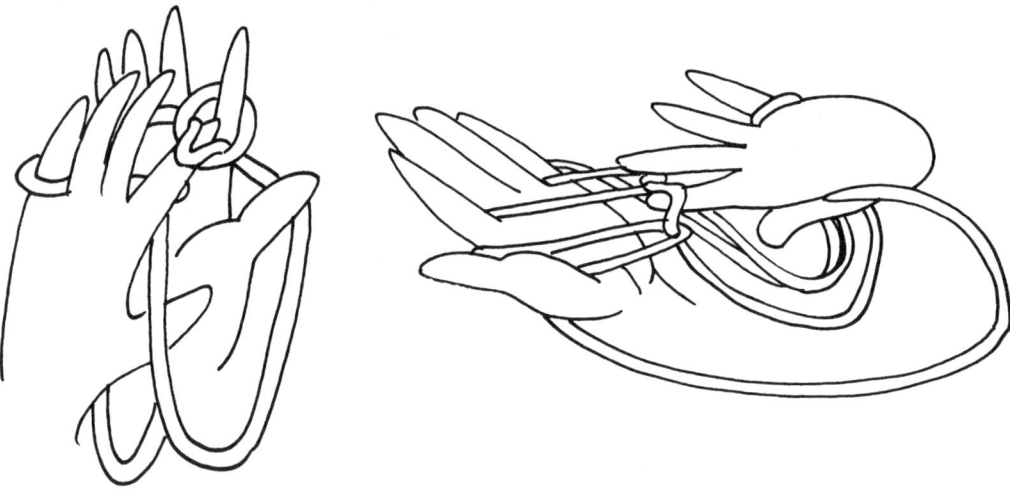

(3) Pull your hands apart, palms facing each other. You now have two crossed strings in the center with two straight strings on each side.

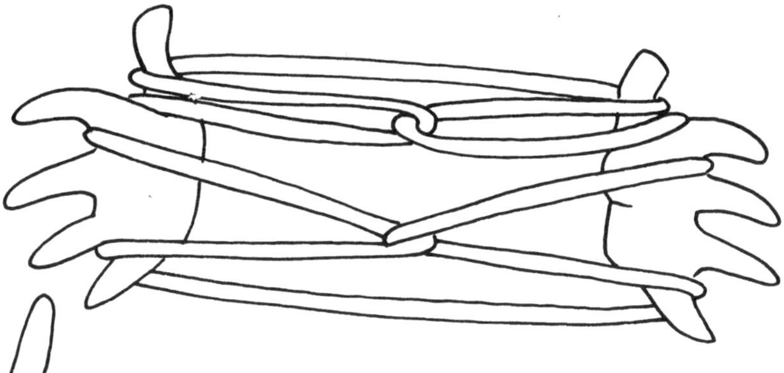

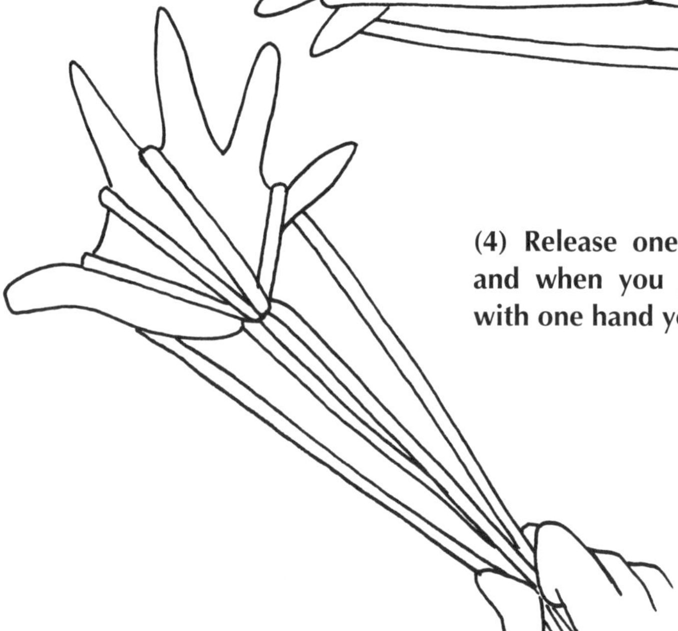

(4) Release one pointer finger loop and when you grasp all the strings with one hand you will see the spear.

TO THROW THE SPEAR

To throw the spear, insert your right pointer finger into the loop around your left pointer finger, from underneath — your palms will touch for a moment. Then release the pointer finger that is part of the spear on your left hand, pull your hands apart, and when you grasp the bottom strings, the spear has moved to your right hand.

You can do this back and forth as often as you want. With practice you will be able to throw the spear quickly.

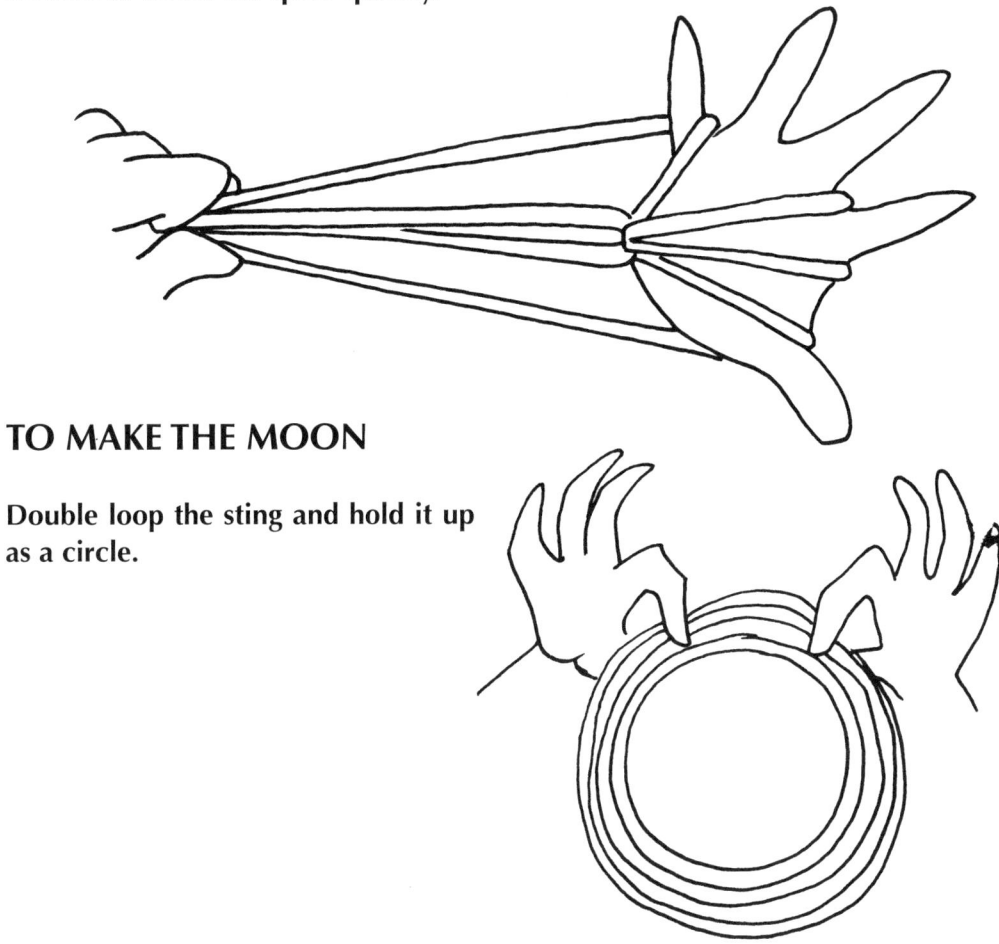

TO MAKE THE MOON

Double loop the sting and hold it up as a circle.

When you are demonstrating string stunts, to be silly you can introduce this shape as "a balloon" — then with a sound effect pop it and watch it deflate.

Collected from Australia and near-by islands in Torres Straits and New Guinea. Also known as "Three Pronged Spear" and in British Columbia as "Pitching a Tent."

TO CREATE CLIMBING TREE

(1) Put the string around your left wrist and then loop it over a second time.

(2) Do the same with the other end of the loop over your right wrist.

(3) Hold your left hand slightly angled above your right hand.

(4) With your right hand take the string that encircles your left wrist and gently pull it down directly into the loop around your right wrist.

(5) Allow the loops to slide off your right wrist. This will create the action of someone climbing a tree.

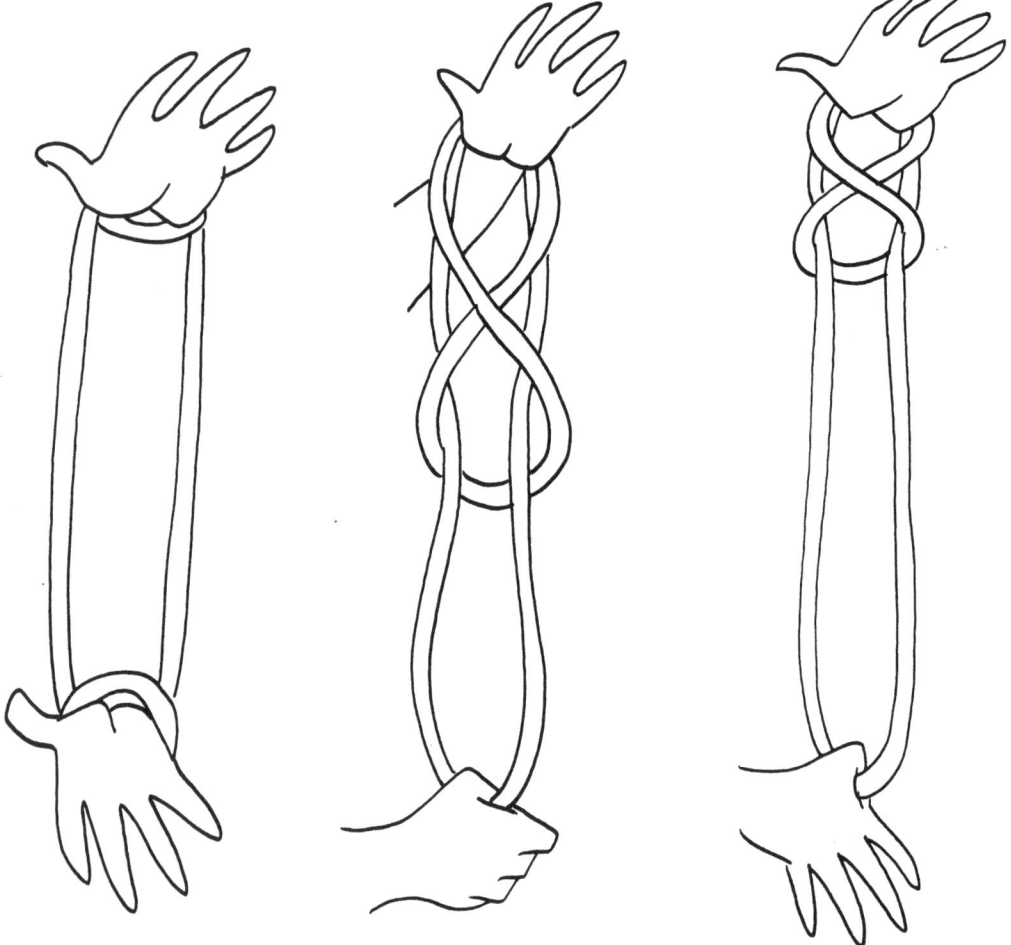

I learned this action figure from David Titus at the 2005 National Storytelling Conference in Oklahoma City, Oklahoma.

TO MAKE THE STAR

(1) Double loop the string as you did to make the moon.

(2) Put this double loop across your left palm with one string going between your thumb and pointer finger and the other between your ring finger and little finger.

(3) Insert the middle finger of your right hand from below into the palmer loop.

(4) Bring your little finger and thumb together (as if they are kissing) over the strings around your right middle finger.

(5) The right hand thumb and little finger — the tips still pressed together — dive behind the strings that are crossing your left palm. As soon as they go under the palmar string, bring these fingers, still holding their string, toward your body. As they come towards you, separate your right thumb and little finger with a slight twisting motion. Your right hand has a loop around the thumb, little finger and middle finger. Your left hand has a loop around your thumb and little finger. As you spread apart your right thumb and right little finger — Voila! A star!

Michael Taylor in *Finger Strings*, calls this "The fastest string figure possible."

This figure was published in The Bulletin of the International String Figure Association in 2001, submitted by Bob Grimes who wrote that his son showed him how to make the star. I learned it from David Titus at the 2005 National Storytelling Conference in Oklahoma City, Oklahoma.

#6
CHOPPING WOOD

STORY

Sure, but it was a long cold winter and Sean's family had no firewood to warm their wee cottage. Then Sean had a bit of luck. A large branch fell from a near-by tree. But there was also a bit of bad luck. The log was too large to fit in his fireplace. To add to his misfortune, his axe was broken. "But our neighbor has an axe," Sean told his wife. He went to the neighbor. "May I borrow your axe?" The neighbor agreed. "Sure, Sean, you can borrow my axe. What a lucky man you are. We haven't a bit of wood ourselves." Sean took that axe. The wood was split. (Do the chopping action here) Aye, but you can be sure Sean was happy. He took half of the log into his house. And when he took the axe back to his neighbor, he gave him the other half of the log. That night there were two warm and happy families by the Irish sea. Now doesn't that warm the cockles of your heart?

STORY BY RUTH STOTTER

DIRECTIONS:

(1) Put the string loop over both thumbs so the strings make a loop in front of you.

(2) Both little fingers come forward and take both strings back with them.

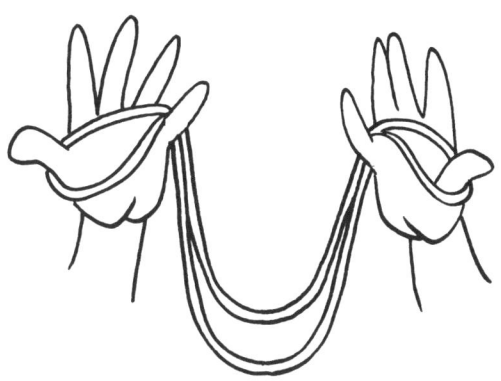

(3) Your right hand pointer finger goes under the left palmar strings and brings them back.

(4) Your left hand pointer finger goes under the right palmar strings and brings them back.

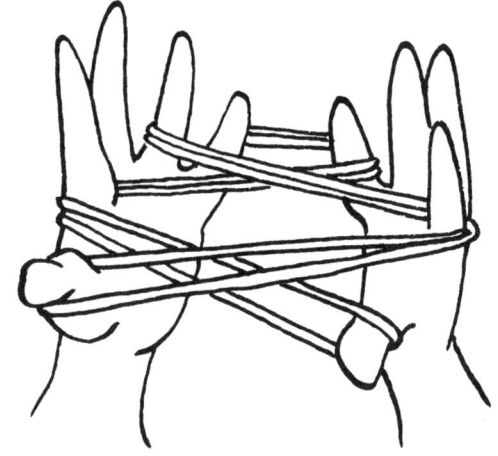

(5) Like sharing the loop, your right thumb goes under the two strings that encircle the right hand pointer finger.

(6) Your left thumb goes under the two strings that encircle the left hand pointer finger. Both thumbs now have their original string and a double string on top.

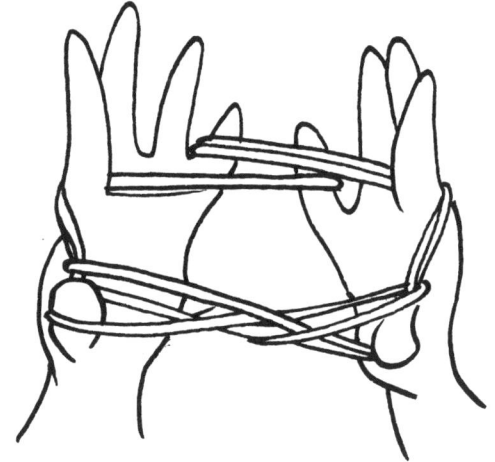

(7) Navajo. Lift the original single string on the bottom of your thumb up and over the double strings.

(8) Carefully release the loops from both pointer fingers. Pull your hands apart until there is a small x-shaped knot in the center.

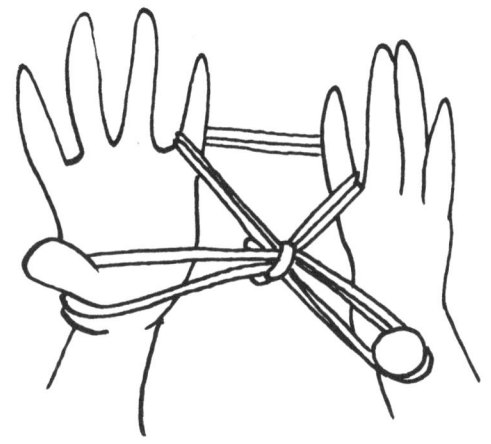

Chopping Wood was collected by Harry and Honor Maude on the Gilbert Islands. I found it in the String Figure Magazine, Volume 6, December 2001.

(9) Release the strings from your thumbs. Turn the figure over so that you are holding the loop in your left hand. The log is at the bottom of the figure. Your right hand will act as the axe.

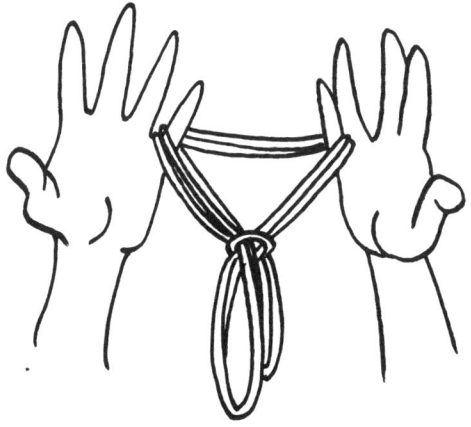

(10) Insert your right hand side-wise into the "V" and make a chopping action. You can accompany this with a sound effect. The knot will disappear and you have two logs.

> In several countries in Africa, people see a man chopping wood with an axe when they look up at the full moon. The story is that he disobeyed a taboo and was put on the moon as punishment. An African man wrote that as a small boy he felt great sympathy for this man condemned to his lunar prison. He was excited when he was ten years old and astronauts went to the moon, certain they would rescue this man. Disappointed not to hear anything on the radio, or read anything in the newspapers, about the man, he realized this was a traditional legend.

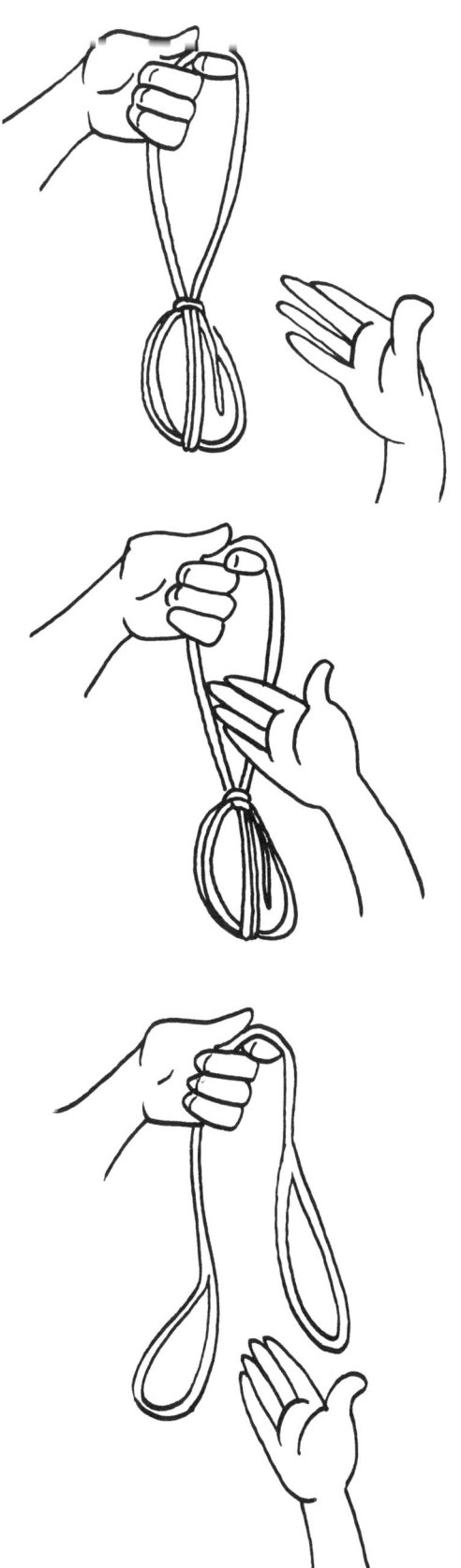

#7
FIREMAN TO THE RESCUE

It is recommended that you use a longer string, a four foot loop, for this story.

> **STORY**
> There was an empty lot and people were building a house. Two little boys climbed on the scaffolding up onto the roof. It began to rain. It rained on one little boy. It rained on the other little boy. The scaffolding was slippery. "Help, help" they called. "Please, someone help us." A fireman came. "Don't be afraid. I brought my ladder." The fireman climbed up the ladder and rescued the two little boys.
>
> **STORY BY RUTH STOTTER**

DIRECTIONS

YOU SAY: *There was an empty lot.*
YOU DO: **Begin opening A. Show the open square.**

YOU SAY: *People were building a house.*
YOU DO: **Complete Opening A.**

YOU SAY: *Two little boys climbed up on the scaffolding to the roof.*
YOU DO: **Bring your little fingers (these are the boys) over the top of all the strings and duck them under the string closest to you. Now carry this string back on your little fingers, portraying their climbing up on the roof.**

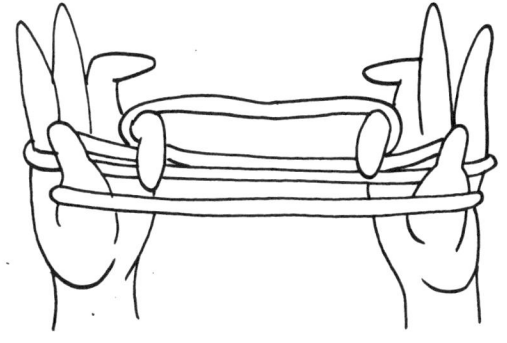

You say: *It began to rain. It rained on one little boy.*

You do: You have two loops around your little fingers. Pull your hands apart so you can identify which is the top string and which is the bottom string. Lift the lower string on one little finger and lift it over the other string. (This move is called "Navajo.") The lower string represents the rain falling on the little boy.

You say: *It rained on the other little boy.*
You Do: The same as above.

DIRECTIONS FOR LADDER

(1) Bend both of your pointer fingers over to hold the string in front of them. You now have a loop on each thumb, two strings between your pointer finger and thumb, your pointer finger is holding a string, and the other strings are in the back.

(2) Continue to hold these firmly.

(3) Identify the straight string that is furthest from you on the outside of your little fingers.

(4) Insert your foot on this string.

(5) Slip your thumbs from their loops.

(6) Continue to hold the loops on your pointer fingers as you release all of the other strings.

(7) Pull slowly on the loops held by your pointer fingers to create climbing the ladder.

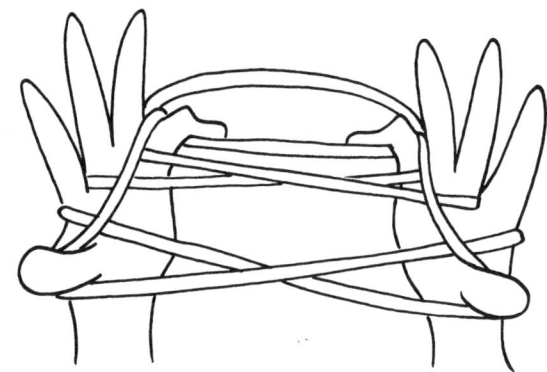
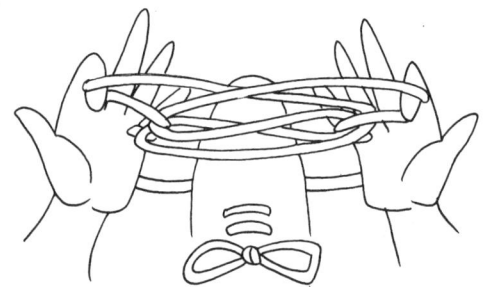
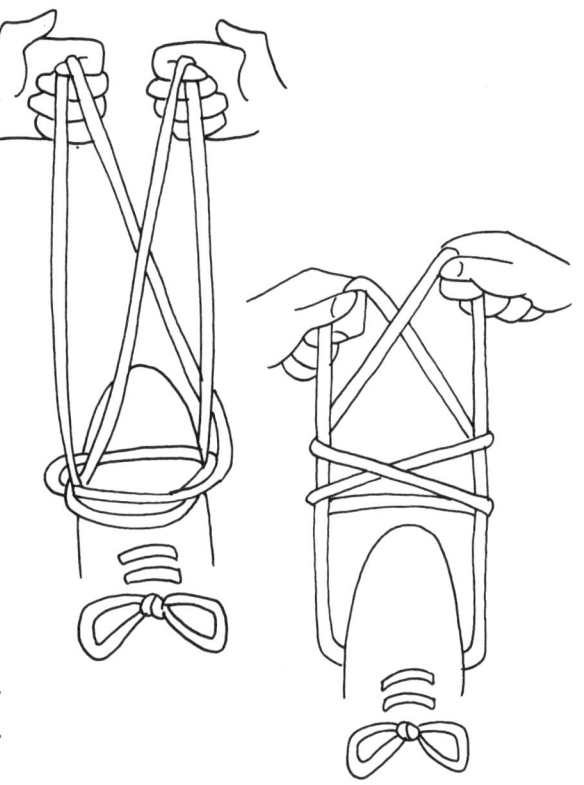

Collected in North Queensland, Australia.

#8 CUTTING THE FINGERS

The special effect will astonish your audience. It's fun to say at the end: "I have to be careful when I do this. Once I cut off all my fingers!"

The following stories use the same string figure directions with minimal variation.

(A) TRAIN STORY
(B) FARMER AND HIS POTATOES
(C) YAM THIEF
(D) CAT AND MOUSE
(E) HOLIDAY STORY ADAPTATIONS
(F) UPROOTING ALOU

DIRECTIONS:

(1) Put the loop of string over your whole left hand with your fingers pointing to the right.

(2) Insert your right pointer finger into the loop, next to the string closest to you. Twist your left pointer finger counter-clockwise and slip the resulting loop over your left hand's pointer finger. Pull on the two strings to create the effect you have tied a knot. You can ask a listener to pull on the two strings to reinforce the idea that this is a tightly tied knot.

(3) Repeat this process, inserting your right pointer finger between your pointer finger and middle finger.

(4) Repeat, inserting your finger between your middle finger and ring finger.

(5) Repeat, inserting your finger between your ring finger and little finger. You now have a loop on your thumb and knots on all four fingers.

(6) To make the magical effect: remove the loop from your thumb and pull the front string toward the right. All the "knots" will disappear, and if you are lucky, you will not lose any fingers!

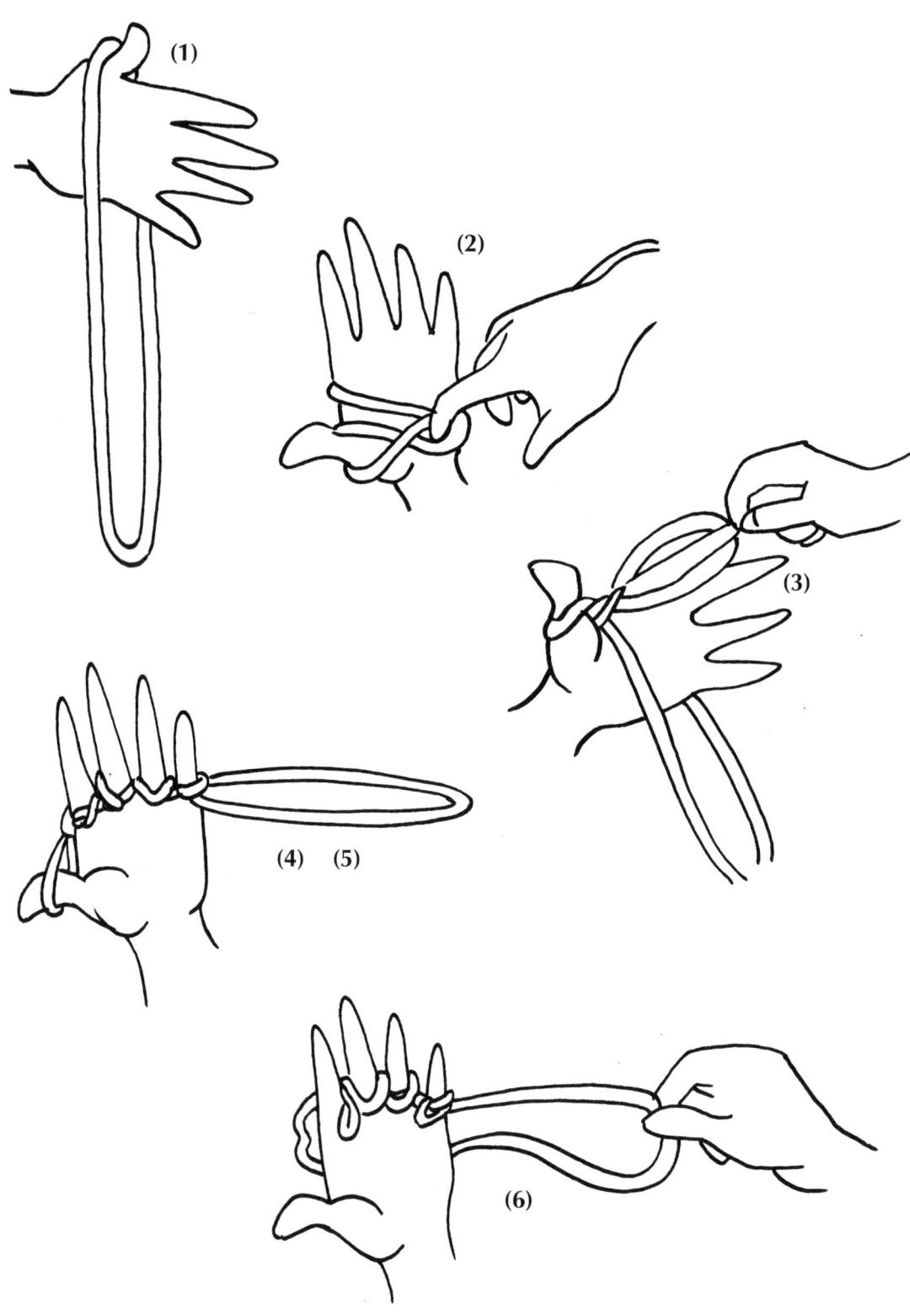

THE TRAIN STORY

In Germany this string stunt is known as The Express Train.

YOU SAY: Here is the locomotive...the engine that pulls the train.
YOU DO: Hold up thumb.

YOU SAY: This is the first class car.
YOU DO: Hold up pointer finger and make the twisted loop that appears to be a knot.

YOU SAY: This is the second class car.
YOU DO: Hold up your middle finger and make another knot.

YOU SAY: This is the dining car.
YOU DO: Hold up your ring finger and make another knot.

YOU SAY: This is the baggage car.
YOU DO: Hold up your little finger and make another knot.

YOU SAY: The engineer says, "All aboard. Let's go!" The train takes off ... and disappears into a tunnel!
YOU DO: As you say this, slip the loop off your thumb and pull the front string to magically release all the knots.

You can add sound effects — a locomotive whistle or the sound of the train chugging away.

The magical effect is achieved as you slowly pull the front string across your palm. The knots on your fingers disappear.

THE FARMER AND HIS POTATOES

A farmer was tying up his bags of potatoes to take to the market. He tied one bag. He tied a second bag. He tied a third bag. He tied a fourth bag. Now the farmer went to get his horse and buggy. When he returned, he took the bags out of his cart to sell at the market.

You say: A farmer was tying up his bags of potatoes to take to the market.
You do: **Hold up thumb.**

You say: He tied one bag.
You do: **After you make the knot, ask an audience member to pull on the two strings so they all can see that the knot is tight.**

You say: He tied a second bag.
You do: **After you make the knot, ask another audience member to pull on the two strings so they can see that the knot is tight.**

You say: He tied a third bag.
You do: **Again, after you make the knot, ask an audience member to pull on the two strings so they all can see that the knot is tight.**

You say: He tied a fourth bag.
You do: **as above**

You say: Now the farmer went to get his horse and buggy. When he returned, he took the bags out of his cart to sell at the market.
You do: **As you say this, dramatically pull the string quickly so that the effect (unlike the train version above where you pull the string slowly) is that the knotted string has magically passed through your fingers.**

THE YAM THIEF

Story: A farmer ties up four bags of his potatoes and a thief runs off with them.

> (You can find this story in *The Story Vine* by Anne Pellowski. New York: Macmillan 1984, pg. 9.)

CAT AND MOUSE

Cat was chasing mice. Cat caught father mouse. Cat caught mother mouse. Cat caught big brother mouse. Cat caught little brother mouse. When little sister mouse cried "You can't catch me!" Cat turned his head to look — and when he did that, all the little mice scampered away!

Put a finger puppet on your thumb and adapt this story for holidays.

HALLOWEEN — Use a witch finger puppet who steals four bags of Halloween treats.

CHRISTMAS — Use a finger puppet wearing a Santa Claus style hat. Introduce him as Santa's helper, and explain that he is tying up the bags so that toys will not spill from the sleigh. Then Santa takes the four bags. Pull the front string as Santa takes off.

ST. PATRICK'S DAY — Use a leprechaun finger puppet. Story: The leprechaun gives four bags of gold to the children (each child is one finger) and tricks them by running off with the bags.

> **Remember to remove the finger puppet from your thumb before you do the magical effect. Or, just before pulling the knots, use your right hand to remove the puppet. If you put the puppet on the thumb of your other hand, you can make it look like the witch or leprechaun is running away with the string.**

UPROOTING ALOU (Alou, also called maniana, is a fungi.)

You say: A man tries to pull up an alou plant. The man pulled on the root.
You do: Make the first knot and pull both strings. The strings will not, of course, release. You can involve the audience by asking them to encourage the man by calling out "Harder! Pull harder."

You say: He tried harder.
You do: Pull on both strings again.

You say: Another man tried.
You do: Make a knot on the next finger. Again, pull both strings.

You say: A woman tried.
You do: Make a knot on the next finger. Again, pull both strings.

You say: Then (the hero of your choice — perhaps a little girl or boy) tries.
You do: This time release your thumb and the strings with their knots will magically release.

(This story was collected in the 1800's from New Caledonia and Loyalty Islands. See *Fun With String Figures* by W. W. Rouse Ball, pg. 49.)

In books featuring string figures, this figure is sometimes called "Thief of Yams". The Quichua Indians of Equador call it "Cutting the Hand". Hawaiians call it "A Gliding Eel." In Burma this stunt illustrates the exploits of a Lushai folk hero. In the Philippines, Africa, and Alaska it is called "Cat and Mouse" and in Germany and Japan it is told as the locomotive or train story. See also *Cat's Cradle and other String Figures* by Joost Elffers & Michael Schuyt. Middlesex, England. Penguin Books. 1978. pg. 44 - 45. For additional variants of "Cutting the Fingers" see *Kwakiutl String Figures* by Julia Averkieva and Mark Sherman, pgs.129, 134. See also "The Yam Thief" in Anne Pellowski's *The Story Vine,* pg. 9-15 and "The Mouse" or "The Yam Thief" in *String Figures* by A. Johnston Abraham, pg. 23-26. Other stories using this figure abound. One tells of four birds who, when frightened, take flight. Additional stories using this string figure can also be found in *Handmade Tales* by storyteller Dianne de Las Casas, Libraries Unlimited, 2008.

#9 SPIDER'S LUNCH

> **STORY**
> Spider was spinning a web, weaving back and forth. Back and forth. Suddenly he heard a sound. BUZZZZZZ. "Oh, good," said Spider, "lunch!"
> When you clap your hands, the mosquito disappears!

DIRECTIONS

YOU SAY: *Spider was spinning a web*
YOU DO: Hold your left palm up with the thumb facing you. Loop the string over your thumb so that it hangs down behind your hand. Insert your left thumb into the bottom of the loop with your thumb pointing toward you. The little finger on your right hand comes over and goes behind the left thumb, hooking under both strings and pulling these strings across the front of your left hand, returning to its original position. You now have two loops around your right little finger and one loop around your right thumb.

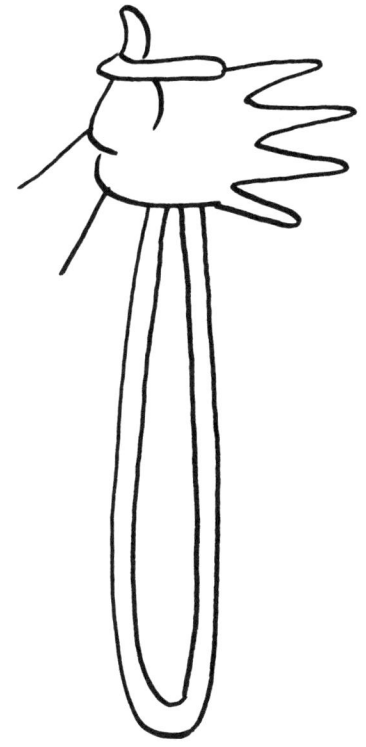

YOU SAY: *Weaving back and forth. Back and forth.*
YOU DO: Your left little finger comes over. Aiming toward your body, this little finger picks up from underneath the two strings on your right thumb and brings these strings with it as it returns to its original position. Your hands are facing each other.

YOU SAY: *BUZZZZZ.* (Mosquito buzzing)
YOU DO: Using your right thumb and pointer finger, slip the double string that is behind your left hand up and over the entire hand. Voila! The mosquito.

You may have to adjust the strings with a tug so that the mosquito is in the center of the strings.

YOU SAY: *Oh, good. Lunch!*
YOU DO: Clap your hands as you release the strings from your little fingers, pull your hands apart, and the mosquito has disappeared!

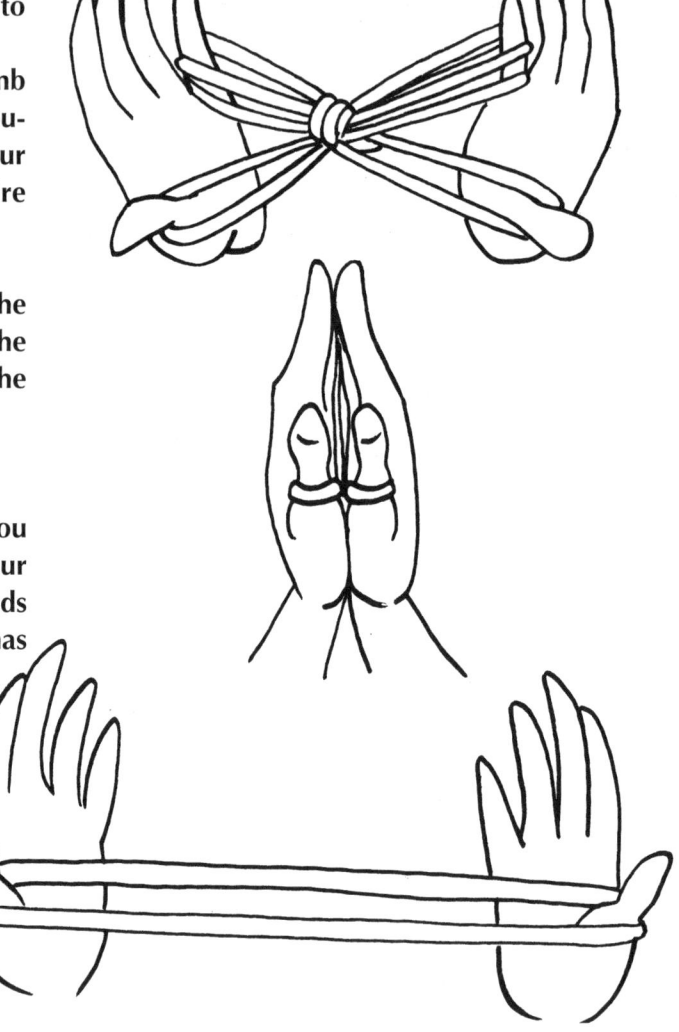

See a similar story that uses this string figure in *The Story Vine* by Anne Pellowski. New York: Macmillan 1984, pg. 5-8. This story is known as, "The Locust" in Ghana, Uganda and by the Melanesians of New Caledonia. It is known as "The Fly" by the Patamana Indians of Guyama.

Storyteller and librarian Jan Seagrave suggests that the teller wear black and use a white string so it really looks like a Spider web. You can also wear colorful clothing and use a black string so the mosquito comes to life.

#10 HOUSE ON FIRE

> **STORY**
>
> There was an empty lot. Some people decided to build a house. Now when you build a house you need a lot of things. They brought in applicances. They brought in a furnace. They put a front door on the house. They put a back door on the house. Finally, they had a lovely house.
>
> One day there was a fire, and they were very glad they had two doors.
>
> One person was able to escape out the front door.
>
> The other person was able to escape out the back door.
>
> TRADITIONAL TALE ADAPTED BY RUTH STOTTER

YOU SAY: *There was an empty lot.*
YOU DO: **Show loop going across both palms as in the beginning of Opening A.**

YOU SAY: *Some people decided to build a house.*
YOU DO: **Complete Opening A.**

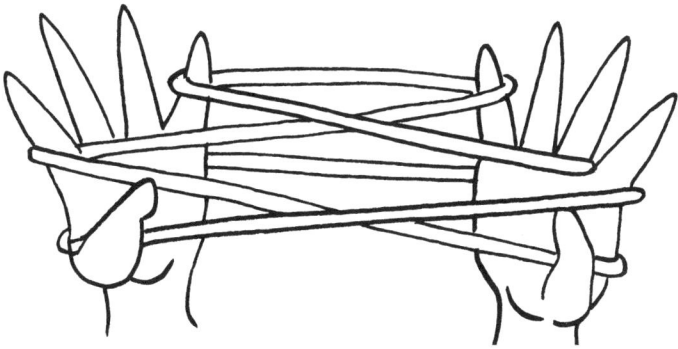

YOU SAY: *Now when you have a house you need a lot of things.*
YOU DO: **Bend down four fingers on both hands to grasp all the strings EXCEPT the front string closest to your body (the thumb loops). Flip this front thumb loop on top, back over all the strings to the back. You will have a large X in the front strings.**

You say: *They brought in appliances. They brought in a furnace.*
You do: **Insert your thumbs into the x (on each side of the crossing strings) and go under all strings to pick up from below the string behind your little finger. Bring this string back toward you, through the "x", to the front. Do this one at a time as you bring in the appliances and furnace.**

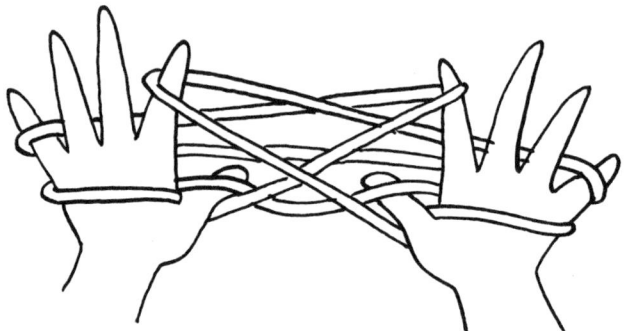

You say: *They put a front door on the house.*
You do: **With your right hand thumb and pointer finger lift the dorsal string (the string behind your palm) from the back of your left hand and bring it to the center.**

You say: *They put a back door on the house.*
You do: **With your left hand thumb and pointer finger lift the dorsal string from the back of your right hand and bring it to the center.**

You say: *Finally they had a lovely house.*
You do: **Palms facing each other, pull your hands apart to create the house.**

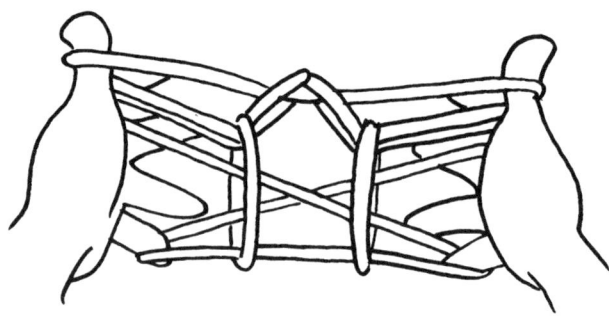

You say: *One day there was a fire, and they were glad they had two doors. There were two people in the house that day.*
You do: **Release the strings from your pointer fingers and slowly spread your hands apart. Two circles will appear between the top and bottom string.**

You say: *One person was able to escape out the front door. The other was able to escape out the back door.*
You do: To make the people run away in opposite directions, slowly com[e] pull your hands apart.

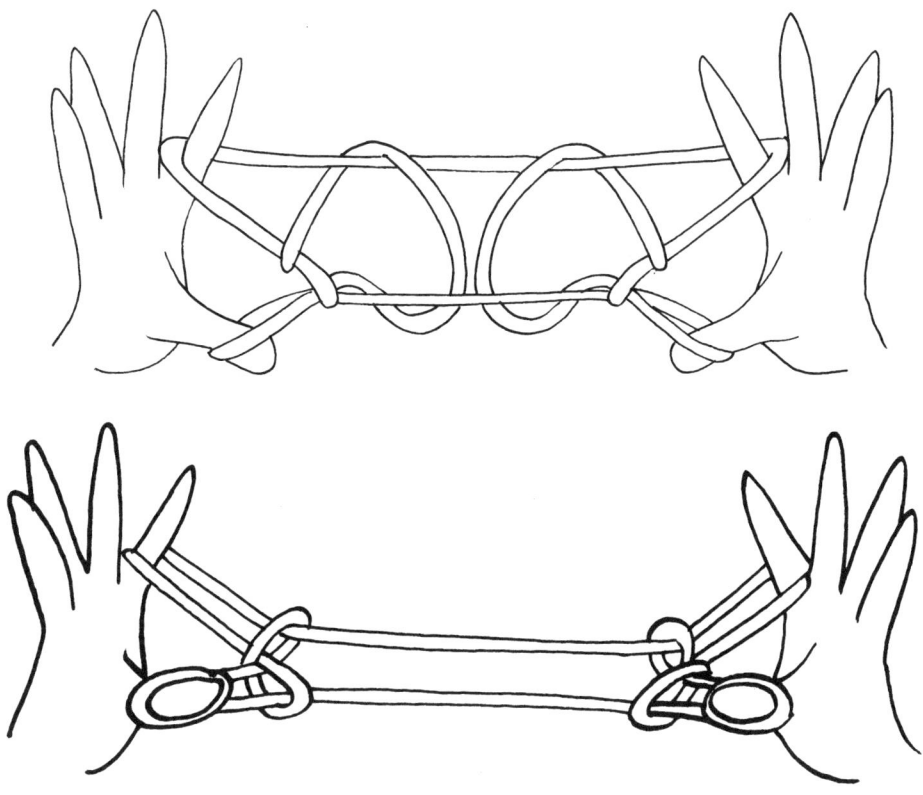

This Inuit Eskimo string figure is called "Siberian House." A chant they recited as they made this figure went something like this: The Tangarot people. We ran away to hide. We made a tent. They ran away." In India they say it was an earthquake that made the two people leave the house.

"A Knotty Story" (following) was collected by David Titus from a native of Savoonga, St. Lawrence Island. Making this figure is described in *String Figure Magazine*. International String Figure Association. Volume 5, March 2000.

#11
A KNOTTY STORY

STORY
A boy had problems. (As you list each problem add a loop on to your pointer finger, following the directions below.) He couldn't find his library book that was overdue. He didn't make the first string of the soccer team. He needed money to fix his bike. He had too much homework. These problems were making knots in his stomach. Then with help from friends and family, all his problems disappeared. And when they did — so did the knots!

DIRECTIONS:

You say: *A boy had problems. (You can create your own character with his or her own problems.)*
You do: **Put the loop in your left hand — holding it in place with your bent over middle, ring and little fingers. Extend your pointer finger and thumb. If you know how to cast on in knitting, make four cast on stitches onto your extended pointer finger. Use your right hand pointer finger, as if it were a knitting needle. Insert your right pointer finger into the loop from behind — your finger comes in pointing toward you. Do a complete couter-clockwise turn with this pointer finger and when you have a loop, slip it on to your left pointer finger. This is knot number one. Repeat this four more times, keeping the loops loose.**

You say: *These were making knots in his stomach.*
You do: **Gently pull out and extend the upper three stitches and slide the bottom stitch up underneath these loops, to the top. Your right hand holds this top loop that you pulled up from below, while your left hand pulls down on the strings. Four knots will appear.**

You say: *Then after awhile, slowly, all his problems disappeared. And when they did — so did the knots!*
You do: **To make the knots disappear, open the loop from the bottom and pull the two strings apart.**

#12
SNAKE'S LUNCH

STORY

One day Snake was hungry. Then Snake saw Lizard, and, remember, Snake was hungry. Quickly, Snake wrapped himself around Lizard. Lizard was caught! But Lizard. did not want to be Snake's dinner. So Lizard wiggled a little and when he twisted, he got away!

DIRECTIONS:

YOU SAY: *Snake was hungry.*
YOU DO: **Hold left hand in front of you, palm facing down, fingers together and slightly cupped, pointing to the right. Loop the string over your left hand, so that it is hanging down. This is Snake.**

YOU SAY: *Snake saw Lizard, and, remember Snake was hungry.*
YOU DO: **Right hand is Lizard. Hold right hand about chest high with fingers facing to the left.**

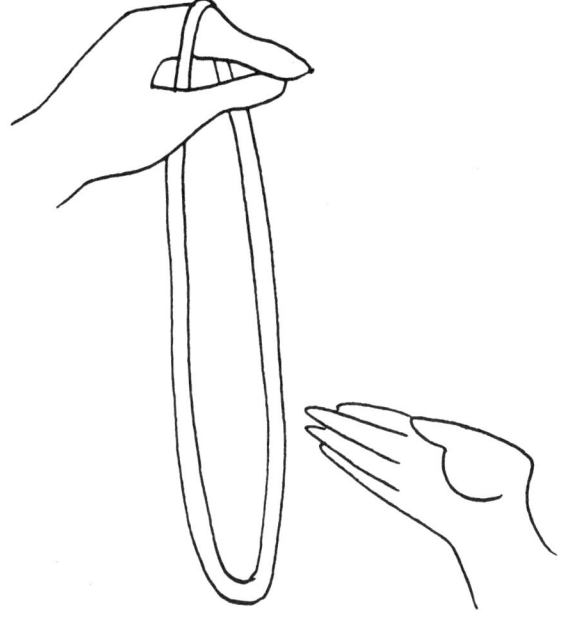

In *The Story Vine,* Anne Pellowski creates a three part string story, beginning with this stunt that has been collected in the Torres Straits (South Pacific), Marquesas, and in islands northeast of Papua New Guinea. She writes that this type of string stunt was used as a trick by early Hawaiians; they would bet strangers that they could not do it, and as it looked easy, the bet was taken, the victim usually ending up with their hand entangled in the string.

You say: *Snake wrapped himself around Lizard. Lizard was caught!*
You do: To capture Lizard put your right hand in the loop and twist it in a complete circle clockwise so that you end with your right hand fingers pointing to the right. Lizard is caught.

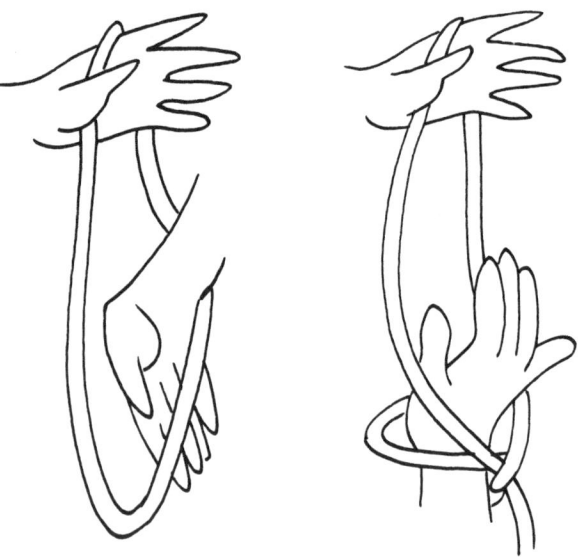

You say: *Lizard. did not want to be Snake's dinner.*
You do: Time for a dramatic pause.

You say: *So Lizard wiggled a little, took a deep breath ...... and got away!*
You do: To escape from Snake: Bring your right hand to your chest so that you can enter the loop hanging from your left wrist directly under your left hand. Pull your hand through the loop (starting on the side closest to your body. Your palms are facing each other) and Lizard has escaped.

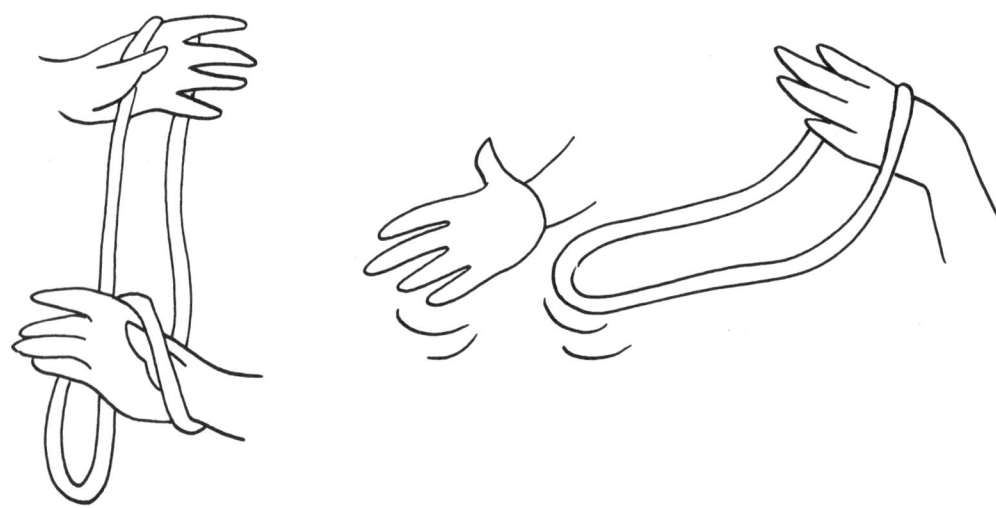

#13 THE CONTEST

This is especially impressive when performed with different color strings for each design. A yellow string for the star, for example. For the old man's winning design, use a multi-colored rainbow string or multi-colored yarn.

> **STORY**
>
> The Emperor announced a contest. Whoever made the most beautiful design using only a piece of string would receive a valuable reward. A little girl made an orange. *(See directions for moon, page 43.)* Her sister made a beautiful star. *(See page 45.)* A little boy made Jacob's ladder. *(See page 37.)* Then an old man, using a rainbow colored string, made this design. It won the contest!
>
> STORY BY RUTH STOTTER

DIRECTIONS

(1) Put the string across your palms, between thumb and little finger and hold them upright, facing each other.

> This string figure is called "Apache Door," but it is also known as "Tent Door" and "Fish-Net". Usually identified as a Navajo string figure, "Apache Door" is performed by many Indian tribes in North and South America.

(2) Put your entire right hand inside the palmar string on your left hand from the bottom up.

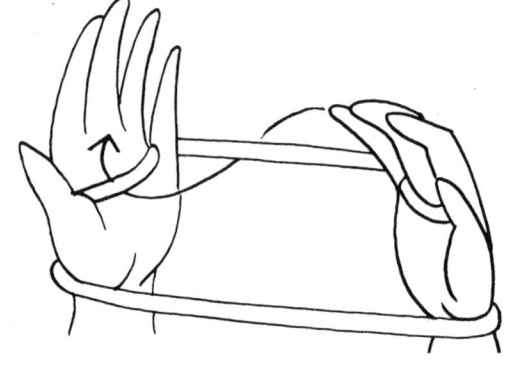

(3) Put your entire left hand inside the right hand's palmer string, from the bottom up.

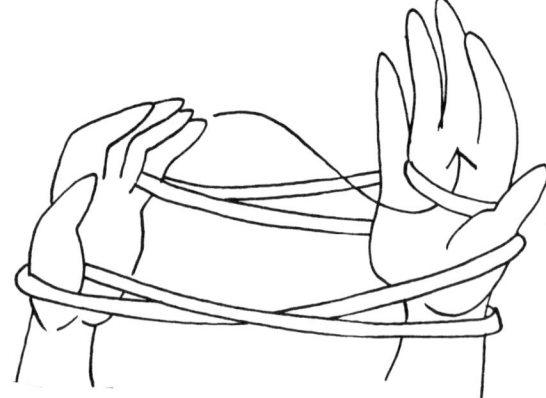

(4) Pull you hands apart.

(5) Use your thumbs to pick up strings closest to you (near little finger strings) on your little fingers.

(6) Use your little fingers to pick up the strings furthest from you (far thumb strings) on your thumb.

(7) Grab all the strings in the center with your right hand and take them between your thumb and pointer finger.

(8) Holding the double loop on your left thumb, pull it up, bringing your thumb toward you (in front of all of the strings), and then reinsert your thumb into the double loop.

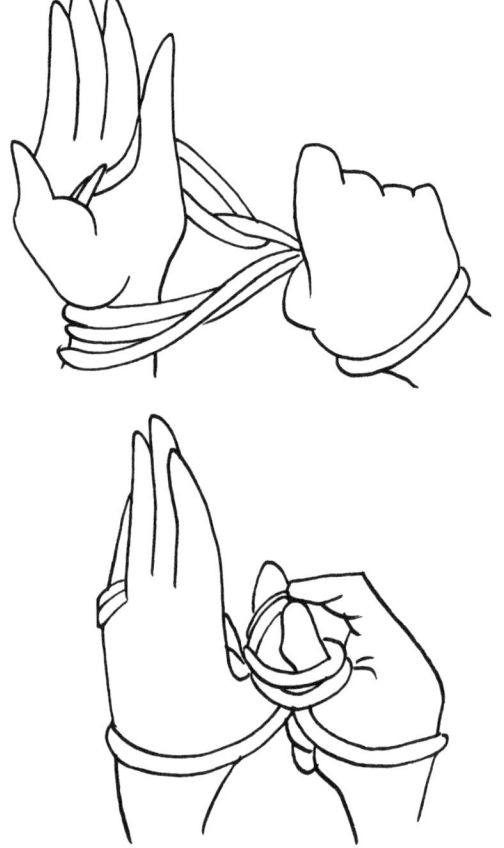

(9) Do the same thing with the double loop on your right thumb.

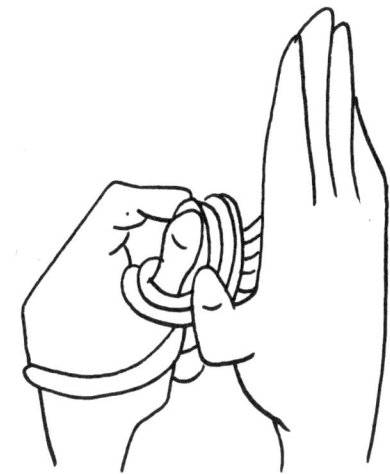

(10) Carefully lift and remove the dorsal string on your right hand (the string that goes behind your hand.)

(11) Carefully lift and remove the dorsal string from your left hand.

(12) Put your hands together and blow magic breath into the strings. (This is part of the traditional mystery of this string figure, so please do not skip it.)

(13) Pull your hands apart and voila! There is the beautiful string figure.

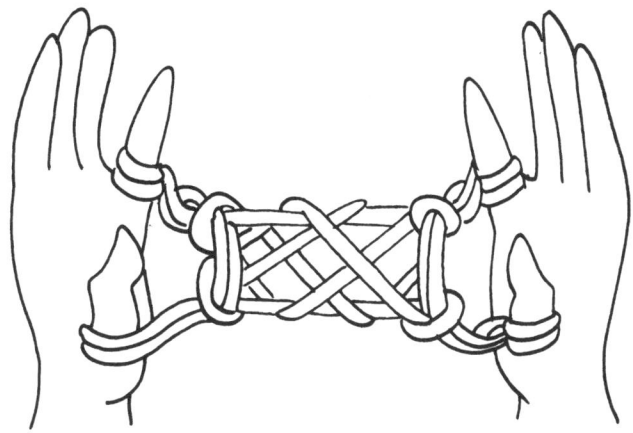

#14 STRING STORY FOR ARBOR DAY

This is easy to translate into other languages. See reference below for Spanish, French, Italian, German, Norwegian, Filipino and Russian translations.

STORY

There was a hole in the ground. A seed was planted. Roots grew. The roots spread out and grew strong. And there was a tree!

STORY BY RUTH STOTTER

DIRECTIONS

YOU SAY: *There was a hole in the ground.*
YOU DO: **Put the loop of string on your left hand with one string between your thumb and pointer finger and the other between your middle and ring fingers.**

YOU SAY: *A seed was planted.*
YOU DO: **With your right hand, enter the loop from the back. Use your right pointer finger to take a hold of the piece of string behind your pointer and middle fingers and pull it all the way down.**

You say: *Roots grew.*
You do: **Again, use your right hand to come into the bottom of the loop. This time take a hold of both strings that are between your pointer and middle fingers. Pull them forward, over the string in front of them and all the down inside the loop.**

You say: *The roots spread out and grew strong.*
You do: **Separate the hanging loops (which represent the roots), putting one on your thumb and one on your little finger.**

You say: *And there was a tree!*
You do: **Turn your hand so the back of your hand faces up. Slowly pull the cross string — the one on top over the cluster of strings until a tree appears.**

Originally published in *Holiday Stories All Year Round: Audience Participation Stories and More,* **edited by Violet Teresa deBarba Miller. Libraries Unlimited. 2008.**

#15 FROG

Use a very large loop — 5 meters or nine feet — and, to add to the effect, double strength green yarn or soft green rope.

THE PRODIGAL FROG

In a land a long, long way from here, a land of palm trees and beautiful beaches, there once lived a little frog. *(Make steps 1-5 from the instructions and hold the string in place.)*

One day the little frog's father said, "Well, little frog, now that you are twelve years old, it is time for you to help in the food garden."

But the little frog was lazy and said, "I won't."

So his father said, "If you do not help in the garden, there is no food for you."

That night the little frog went hungry. *(Move your hands slightly upwards, playing the rope slowly through your fingers to hold the 'frog' shape as he becomes a little thinner.)*

The next day the father again asked, "Little frog, come and work in the garden."

Little frog said, "No." And again he had no dinner.

As this went on day by day little frog grew thinner and thinner. *(Move the hands up to make the thin frog.)*

Then little frog had an idea. "I will go to the next village. They will give me something to eat." When the people saw how thin he was, they gave him dinner. He grew fatter. *(Move your hands down and apart so he gets fatter.)*

The next day he ate and ate and grew very fat. *(Move your hands down and apart to enlarge the frog so the center of the design fattens.)*

Then the people said, "We have always wanted a garden. Little frog, go outside, dig up the earth and start a garden for us."

Little frog said "No."

That night they did not give him dinner and he grew thinner. The next day and the next he had no food, and he grew so thin, you could see right through him. *(Show this)*

The next day little frog went home. His father ran to meet him and cuddled him. He gave him a delicious welcome home dinner. Then little frog said, "Father, I am glad to be home. And I will work in the garden." And after that, he worked in the garden every day, and he ate every day, so he never got fat again *(show)* and he never got too thin *(show)*. He was just right!

"PRODIGAL FROG" STORY CREATED BY PHILIP DAVID NOBLE.

The traditional frog designs were taught to Noble in Safoa, Northern District Papua New Guinea, in 1973 accompanied by a short story about frog visiting his grandmother. Ruth Stotter modified the tale by inserting the village.

FROG OLYMPICS

⌘ : When you see this sign, make Fydor small and then pull on the strings to make him stretch him out to jump.

When the frogs decided to hold an Olympic competition, Fydor Frog was excited. He signed up to enter the lily pad leaping event, and he practiced every day ... first scrunching himself and then stretching out to make a great leap. ⌘ Over and over he practiced. ⌘ Finally the day of the event came. That morning he had a healthy breakfast. A mosquito *(see page 60 if you want to make this here)* and a butterfly *(see pages 21 and 22 if you want to make these here)*. For the opening ceremony there was a long line of frogs, and each was told to leap over the frog in front of him ⌘ and then crouch low for the next frog to leap over him. ⌘

The lily pad contest was the very first competition and there was a large crowd. Everyone cheered (encourage your listener(s) to cheer) when Fydor stepped out and took a bow. He swam out to the first lily pad. A Canadian goose gave the opening honk to begin. But Fydor could not move. He was stage-struck with all those people watching. He sat there. The crowd waited. Then they shouted, "Come on Fydor. You can do it. Jump!" But he couldn't move. He sat there as if frozen on the lily pad. Then the closing honk came and his time was up. However, just then, with a great leap ⌘ he jumped to the next lily pad. And then he jumped ⌘ the one after that. ⌘ And then the third and final one. ⌘ When the end of the event came it was clear that Fydor had made better time than anyone else. But because he did not leap in his assigned time slot, the judge said "Rivet...rivet. Disqualified."

But, I am happy to tell you — Fydor didn't care. He knew he had been faster than all the other frogs. He went home ⌘ a happy frog and he continued leaping back and forth all the rest of his life. Like this. ⌘

STORY BY RUTH STOTTER

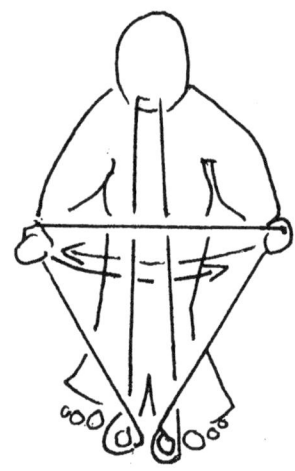

(1) Put one end of the loop in your mouth. Stretch it to go between your big toe and middle toe and let the rest of the loop lie on the ground.

(2) Pick up the loop from the floor in each hand — making a loop on each side. Take these loops around and behind (not through) your toe-mouth loop and cross them.

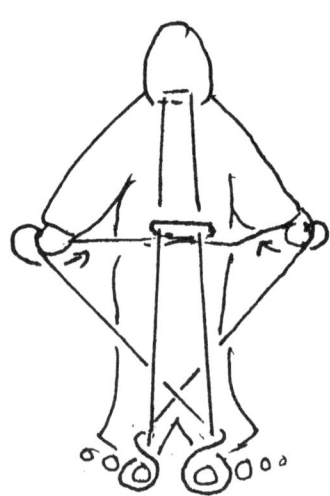

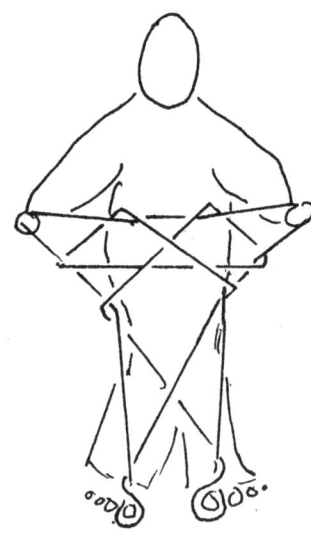

(3) Put your hands through these loops so the string rests on your elbows.

(4) Now take hold of end of the loop that is in your mouth in both hands.

(5) Let the loops on your elbows slide off over this string.

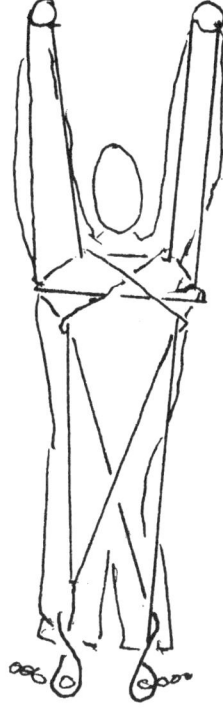

(6) Move your hands together up over your head to stretch the frog and make him thin.

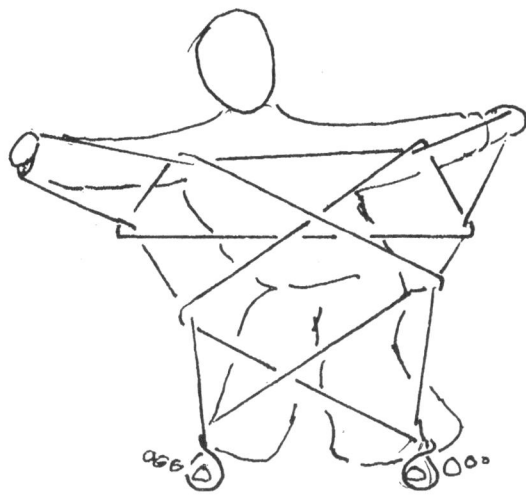

(7) Move your hands apart and down for the fat frog.

#16 ZEN STORY

STORY

Nan-In, a Japanese Zen master, received a visitor seeking guidance, wanting to learn the Zen philosophy. He told Nan-In about himself, his work, his studies, and what he planned to do with his life. Nan-In served tea. *(Do steps 1-3.)* He poured his visitor's cup full, but kept right on pouring. Tea overflowed onto the embroidered cloth covering the table. *(Do step 4 and then raise your hands in shock as you become the visitor.)* The would-be student could not restrain himself. "My cup was full, yet you kept on pouring. Why?"

"Like this cup," Nan-In replied, "You are full of your expectations and ideas. How can you learn Zen unless you first empty your cup."

TRADITIONAL ZEN STORY

DIRECTIONS:

(1) Place the loop over your left thumb and pointer finger with the loop handing down behind your hand.

(2) Lift the loop up and let it fall behind your hand, between your left thumb and pointer finger.

(3) With your right thumb and pointer finger take a hold of the bottom of the hanging loop and lift it up. Let your left thumb and pointer finger come together to hold these strings and let the loop hang down.

(4) Turn your hand so your fingers point toward the floor to create the illusion that this is a tea-pot. Take hold of the loop and start out gently and then pull with a flourish as you "pour the tea."

#17 BUTTONHOLE TRICK

DIRECTIONS:

(1) Put the loop of string into a buttonhole on a shirt or jacket you are wearing. Hold the sting on both thumbs.

(2) Put your little finger of right hand under the loop that is around your left thumb and bring it back to your original hands apart position.

(3) Hook the little finger of your left hand under the loop that is around your right thumb and bring it back to your original hands apart position.

(4) Slip your right thumb out of its loop and put it through the loop held by right little finger.

(5) When you let the left little finger release its string and pull your hands apart the string will appear to have magically passed through your buttonhole!

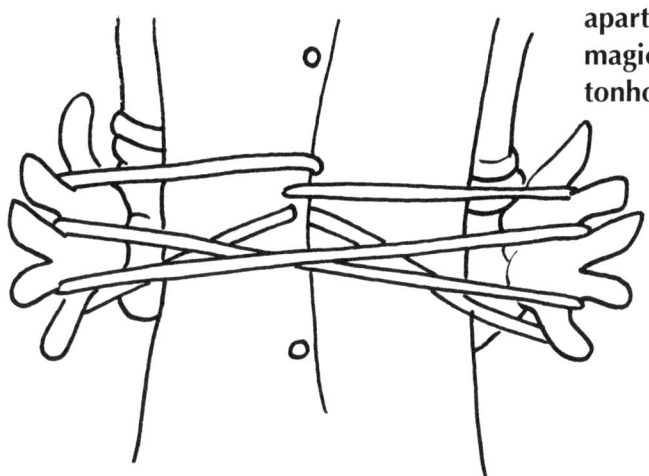

ANOTHER BUTTON HOLE TRICK

Put the loop through your buttonhole. Do Opening A. Now drop the strings from your thumbs. When you drop the string from your left pointer finger and the right little finger loop at the same time, the string is magically free!

To buttonhole someone: This expression from the last century was used to express grabbing someone by their top button and not letting them go until they listen to what you have to say.

#18 RING STUNT

You can use your loop of string to do this magic trick. It is recommended that you ask an audience member if they will let you use their ring so that there is no suspicion you are using a specially designed trick ring.

(1) Insert the ring into the doubled loop.

(2) Put the string in your hands in preparation for Opening A.

(3) Do Opening A with your middle finger.

(4) Ask an audience member to cup their hands under the strings to catch the ring.

(5) To obtain the maximum effect, practice this until you can do it quickly.

    1) Release the string from both little fingers.

    2) Release the string from the middle finger of your left hand.

    3) Release the string from the thumb on your right hand.

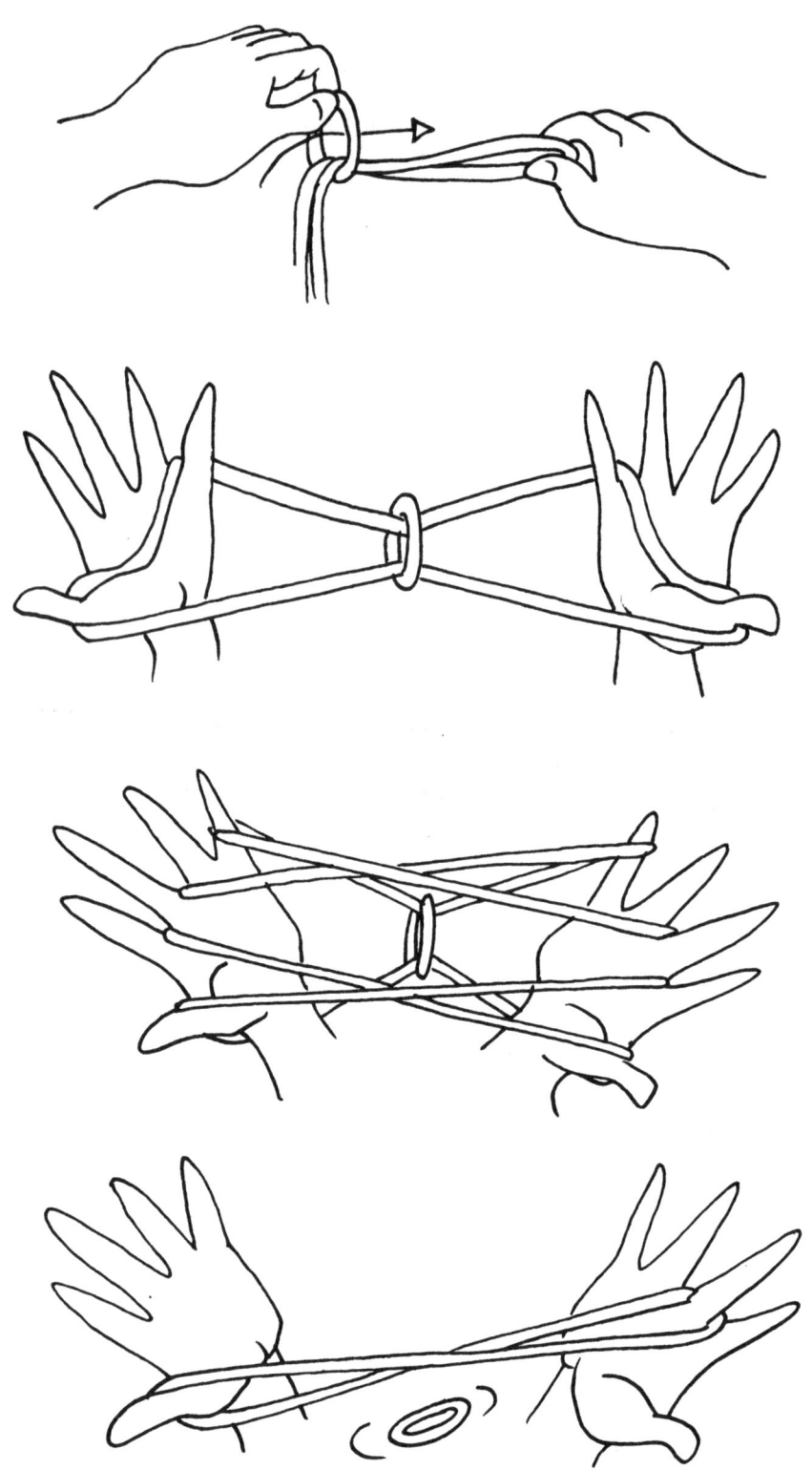

#19 STRING STUNT FOR TWO PEOPLE

This is fun to use as an ice-breaker or party-game.

DIRECTIONS

Each person has a partner. Give each couple two strings. Ordinary packaging string or yarn is fine. Each person's string should be about eight feet in length. One person ties each end of their string to their wrists. The second person ties the string around one wrist, then crosses it under their partner's string before tying the other end of their string to their other wrist.

When all the couples are ready tell them that there is a way to separate the two strings without removing them from their wrists. They will step over and under the strings, trying to figure it out.

I suggest saying: If someone has done this before, please go into another room to execute the separation; do not give it away.

Allow the pair or pairs participating about five minutes to try to figure it out. The longer string encourages them to step over and under their strings in their creative attempts to solve the puzzle.

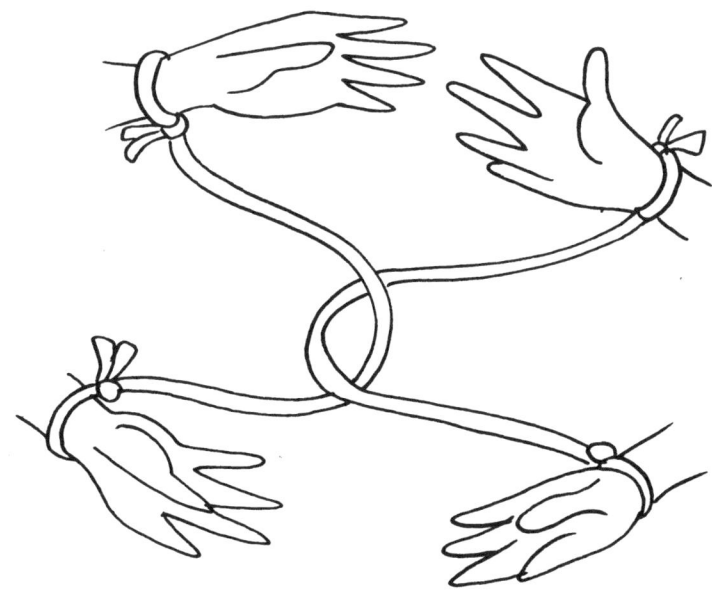

THE SOLUTION: One person holds one of their wrists with the palm facing up. The second person (you) makes a loop with your string, making this loop from the back of the cross, on your partner's side of the crossed string. Slide this loop under your partner's wrist string - with their palm facing up. After the loop is pulled all the way off the other persons hand, the strings will have separated.

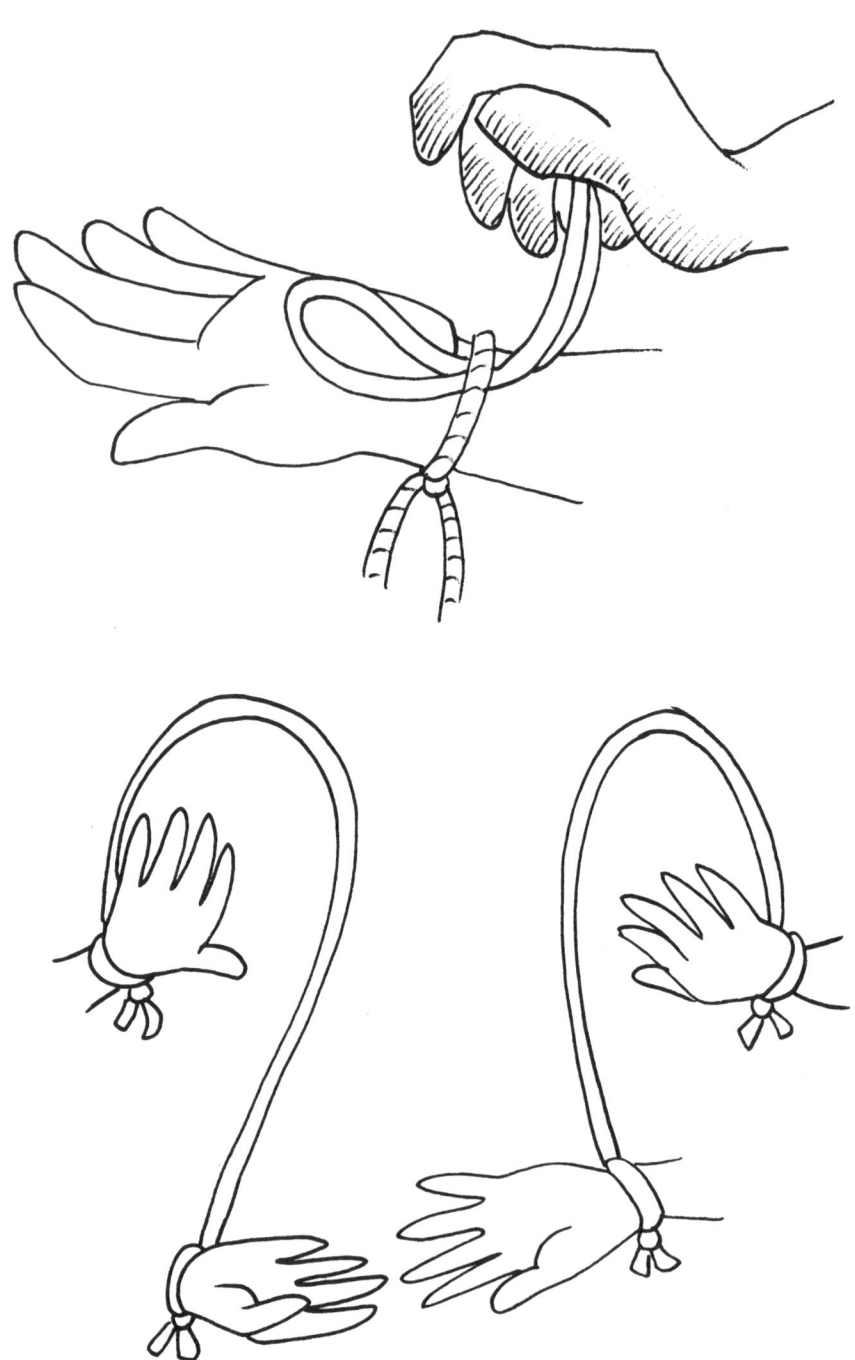

#20 STRING JOKE

Use three straight pieces of string. They can be different colors to literally add color to the joke.

STORY

Three strings stood outside an ice-cream store that had a sign, "No Strings served here." One of the strings said, "I think I will give it a try." The string entered the store and the man behind the counter said, "Didn't you see the sign? We don't serve strings here." The string turned around and left. "I'm going to give it a go, " the second string said. But the same thing happened. The man behind the counter glared at him. "We don't serve strings here." He left. The third string doubled himself over and under and up again. Then he tore open his top, spreading small pieces of string about. *(Do this ... tie a knot in the string and open up the top, spreading out the string fibers.)* When he entered the ice-cream store the man looked at him hard and long. "Aren't you a string?" he finally asked. The string replied, "No, I am afraid not." ("No, I am a frayed knot.")

#21
STRING GAME

For 2 to 6 players

DIRECTIONS

Place the string as a large circle or loop on the floor, ground or a table. Take turns putting an item into the loop. When you put an item in, it is not allowed to touch any other item. If it does, you are eliminated. You can do this out-of-doors with nature items, use buttons, or any other objects.

This string game was created by Mike Spiller (Houston, TX). See his web site: www.physiciansofphun.com.

Terminology & Basic Moves

OPENING A:
This is used in making many string figures. (The game "Cat's Cradle" begins with Opening A.)

DIRECTIONS:
Put one end of your loop of string between the thumb and little finger on your left hand so you have a palmar string. Put the other end of the loop between your right hand thumb and little finger, so you have a palmar string on both hands. Now pick up the left palmar string with the pointer finger on your right hand and the right palmar string with your left hand pointer finger. This is opening A.

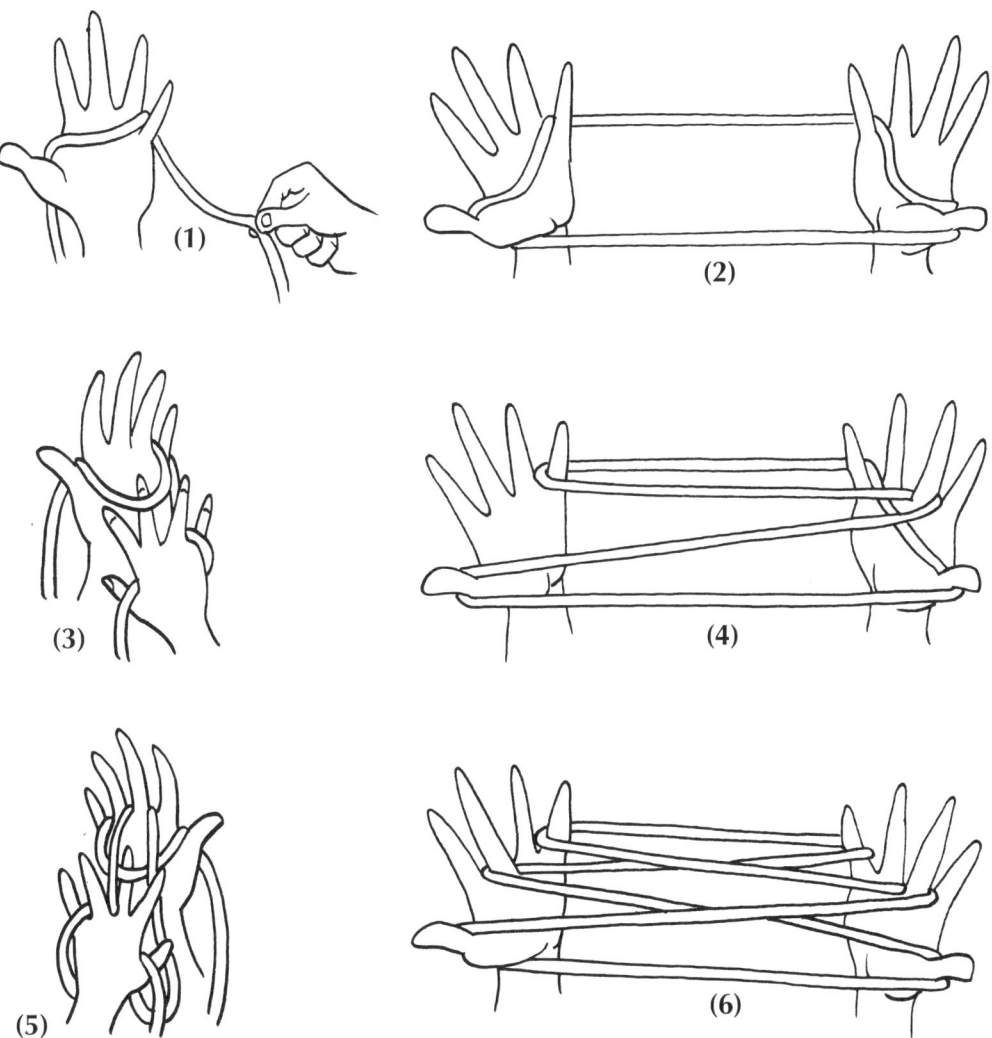

YOUR FINGERS
String books use different names for the fingers. This book uses thumb, pointer finger, middle finger, ring finger and little finger. In other publications the pointer finger may be called the index finger. The little finger may be called the pinky or baby finger.

NAVAJO
With two or more strings on one finger, lift the lower string up over the bottom string on the same finger. You can use your fingers or teeth to Navajo.

SHARING A LOOP
Extend the loop so that it is over both the original finger as well as the new finger or thumb you have added. You can use your fingers or teeth to move the string.

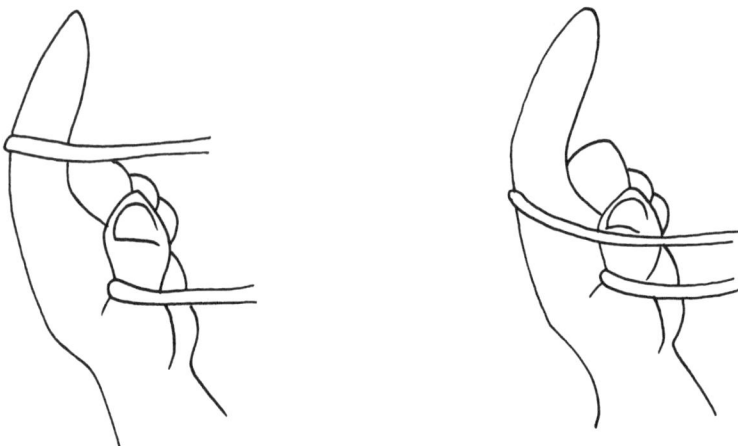

PALMAR STRING
The string lying across the front of your palm.

DORSAL STRING
The string going across the back of the hand.

NEAR STRING
If the directions say "near little finger string" that means that there is a loop around the little finger and you are to move the string that is closest to you.

FAR STRING
If the directions say "far thumb string" that means that there is a loop around the thumb and you are to move the string on the thumb that is furthest from you.

Additional String Stories

"The Pesky Skeeter," "Fox Chases Bunny," "The Worm," "The Stubborn Turnip," in *Handmade Tales: Stories to Make and Take* by Dianne de Las Casas. Libraries Unlimited: Westport, Connecticut, 2008.

"Planting a Tree" — a string story for Arbor Day. Original story by Ruth Stotter. *Holiday Stories All Year Round: Audience Participation Stories and More,* edited by Teresa Miller. Libraries Unlimited, 2008. The story is translated into French, German, Italian, Spanish, Norwegian, Russian and Filipino.

"Candle Caper" story in Anne Pellowski's *The Story Vine*, 1984. Also in *The World's Best String Games* by Joanmarie Kalter. New York: Drake Publisher, 1978, pg. 92.

String Figures and Stories on DVD and VHS

Hawaiian String Figures. Lois and Earl Stokes. www.stringfigure.com

The Healing Art of String Figures. Lois and Earl Stokes. www.stringfigure.com

How To Make the Dog and Other Fun String Tricks by Anne Glover: info@anne-glover.ca. www.anneglover.com. 250-360-2101.

The Monkey's Heart: An Innovative Tool for Learning French Through String Stories. Anne Glover. Story String Productions. www.anneglover.ca/. 250-360-2101.

Sharing with String Through String Ministries. David Titus. String Figure Store. 130 SW"B" Avenue. Lawton, OK 73501. Stringfigurestore.com/

String Fun with the Parables. David Titus. String Figure Store. 130 SW"B" Avenue. Lawton, OK 73501. Stringfigurestore.com/

String Magic from Around the World with David Titus. 1997, 2005. String Figure Store. 130 SW"B" Avenue. Lawton, OK 73501. Stringfigurestore.com/

String Things: Stories, Games and Fun! With Barbara G. Schultz-Gruber. Available from BGSG Storytelling. 1995. 2855 Kimberly. Ann Arbor, Michigan 48104.

David Novak tells "Jack and the Beanstalk" with string on *Tell Me A Story,* volume 1 — Hometown Entertainment. 800-786-7983. (Recorded at 1995 National Storytelling Association Festival.)

Where to Find Strings

Ordinary yarn and string tied with a square knot (see below) to form a loop will make most of the string figures in this book. However, colored string, multicolored string or multicolored yarn will create beautiful effects.

Experiment with different types of string as some string figures can be created more easily using a string that offers tighter tension while others work better with a more flexible string.

To make a loop from a fibre cord, join the ends with heat from a match or candle.

> **In traditional string figure art the string is derived from plant fiber, such as hibiscus cord, leather thongs, fish line or animal guts. Human hair has also been used.**

To tie a square knot, start out as if you are tying a shoe, making sure that you put the right side of the string over the left. Then repeat, but this time put the left string over the right. Pull the strings so the knot is tight. Cut off any protruding ends.

Where To Purchase Strings

DAVID TITUS
PO Box 1406
Lawton, OK 73502-1406
Phone 580-353-4710
Okteller@juno.com
www.storyteller-Wordsmith.com

Titus's strings are fused (no knot) nylon and come in assorted bright colors. They are available in two lengths- the standard is 65" and the long is 72". Current prices are $.50 standard or 25 stings for $9.00; 50 for $16.00; 100 (in container) $35.00. Longer length strings are 110 strings for $35.00. Plus shipping.

TALIB AND OLIVIA HUFF
Phone 916-484-0606
ohuff@dcn.org
Multi-colored rainbow loops, approximately one yard. Current prices 1-19 loops: $3.00 each. 20-79 $2.50 each. 80 +: $2.00 each. Plus shipping and applicable taxes.

LOIS AND EARL STOKES
www.stringfigure.com

RR2 Box 4040
Pahoa, Hawaii 96778-9722
808-965-1345

*Bag of five shorter shiny rainbow strings —
$5 plus shipping.*

Children's Books That Feature String Figure Art

Lost: A Story in String by Paul Fleishman. Henry Holt Publishers, 2000.

A Piece of String is a Wonderful Thing by Judy Hindley. Illustrated by Margaret Chamberlin. Candlewick Press, New York, 1993.

Recommended String Figure Books

Abraham, A. Johnston. *String Figures*. Algonac, Michigan: Reference Publications, Inc. 1988.

Averkieva, Julia and Mark Sherman. *Kwakiutl String Figures* by Seattle. University of Washington Press, 1992.

Ball, W. W. Rouse. *String Figures*. New York: Dover Publications, Inc., 1971.

Biddle, Steve and Megimi. *Magical String*. London: A Beaver Book, 1990.

De Witt, Sorena. *String Figures from Around the World*. Torrance, California: Heian International, Inc., 1995.

Elffers, Joost and Michael Schuyt. *Cat's Cradle and other String Figures*. Middlesex, England. Penguin Books, 1978.

Gryski, Camilla. *String Games*. New York: William Morrow and Company,1983. *Many Stars and More String Games* by Camilla Gryski. New York: William Morrow and Co., 1985. *Super String Games*. New York: Morrow Junior Books, 1987.

Gupta, Arvind. *String Games*. National Book Trust, A-5 Green Park. New Delhi 110016, India. Illustrations by Avinash Deshpande (Order from indiaclub.com)

Haddon, Kathleen. *Cat's Cradle from Many Lands*. New York: Longman's, Green and Co., 1912.

Holbrook, Belinda. *String Stories: A Creative Hands-On Approach for Engaging Children in Literature*. Washington, Ohio: Linworth Publishing, 2002.

Jayne, Caroline Furness. *String Figures and How to Make Them*. New York: Dover Publishing, 1962. (Reprint of 1906 String Figures published by Charles Scribner.)

Kalter, Joanmarie. *The World's Best String Games*. New York: Drake Publishers, 1978.

Leeming, Joseph. *Fun with String* . New York: Dover Publications, 1974.

Taylor, Michael. *Pull the Other One!* Hawthorne Press, 2000. *Now You See It. String Games and Stories*. England: Hawthorne Press, 2002. www.hawthornepress.com. *Finger Strings: A Book of Cat's Cradles and String Figures*. Edinburgh: Floris Books, 2008.

Titus, David. *Native American String Figures. African String Figures. Native Alaskan String Figures*. String Figure Store. 130 SW "B" Street. Lawton, Oklahoma. 73501. Stringfigurestore.com/

Pellowski, Anne. *The Story Vine*. New York: Macmillan, 1984.

On the Web

There are dozens of directions for making string figure available on line — often with accompanying videos so that you can watch the string figures being made!

RECOMMENDED

1. Bibliography prepared by Dr. Tom Storer published on the website of the International String Figure Association. www.isfa.org/biblio.htm

2. Kid's Guide to Easy String Figures www.alyson.org/figures/introkids.htm

3. String Games by Arvind Gupta with illustrations by Avinash Deshpande. vidyaonline.org/arvindgupta/stringgames.pdf

4. Michael P. Garofalo — Resources for String Figures. www.gardendigest.com/string/index.htm

Index

Apache Door, 69
Arbor Day, 73, 95

Boas, Franz, 15
Butterfly, 22, 23, 25, 26
Buttonhole stunts, 83

Christmas, 57

Dorsal string, 62, 71, 94

Easter Island, 15

Far string, 94
Finger puppet, 57
Flea, 21, 22,
Frog, 75, 76, 77, 78

Glover, Anne, 7, 96

Halloween, 57
Huff, Talib and Olivia, 98

(ISFA) International String Figure Association, 7, 45, 63, 102, 104

Jacob's Ladder, 37, 38, 69

Ladder, 37, 38, 41, 51, 52, 69
Leprechaun, 57
Lizard, 67, 68

Maui, 15
Moon, 41, 43, 45, 49, 69
Moth, 23

Navajo 15, 23, 38, 39, 48, 52, 69, 94
Near String, 94
Neck Release, 27, 29, 31, 33, 35
Noble, Philip David, 7, 35, 76
Opening A, 23, 25, 26, 33, 37, 39, 41, 51, 61, 83, 85, 93

Palmer string, 25, 70
Pellowski, Anne, 7, 57, 58, 60, 67, 95, 101

Seagrave, Jan, 7, 60
Sharing a Loop, 94
Sherman, Mark, 7, 22, 58, 59, 100, 104
Siberian House, 63
Snake, 67, 68
Spear, 41, 42, 43
Spider, 15, 59, 60
Spiller, Mike, 7, 91
Stokes, Lois and Earl, 96, 98
Square Knot, 97
Star, 41, 45, 68, 69
St. Patrick's Day, 57

Train, 53, 55, 56, 58,
Titus, David, 7, 44, 45, 63, 96, 98, 101

Zen story, 81
Zulu, 23

Now that you are interested in making string figures you will want to join

ISFA
INTERNATIONAL STRING FIGURE ASSOCIATION
Membership : USA $25.00 year (Outside USA $35.00)

WEB SITE:
www.isfa.org

Members receive an annual bulletin, quarterly magazine, ISFA NEWS published twice a year, occasional video clips on CD-ROM and a String Figure of the Month.

To become a member contact:
Mark A. Sherman Ph.D
P.O. Box 5134
Pasadena, CA 91117
626-398-1057
webweavers@isfa.org